AF244092

THE ARCADIA MUSIC FESTIVAL MURDERS

by

Mike Culpepper

Other books by Mike Culpepper

Better Than Starbucks

The Saga of Colm the Slave

The Arcadia Music Festival Murders

copyright 2018 by Mike Culpepper

ISBN: 978-0-9879017-6-7

1

"I'm quitting."

Police Chief Jim Tull shook his head. "You can't do that, Larry. I need you. You know we got this damn thing coming up and you're the only cop around that I can trust to handle it."

"Hire the Mounties."

"Now, Larry, you know Council would never go for that." Tull smiled, "That would take a day's, two days' earnings, easy."

"I can't do it this year."

"Larry, I can't get through this thing without you."

"This thing" was the annual LakeFest Music Festival. Larry hated it. Every year it got bigger. Every year there were problems. Every year the problems got bigger and bigger. Last year was the worst. Larry could still remember the blood in the water, the children screaming… He shuddered and shook his head. "No."

Tull leaned forward. "Larry, that was all my fault. I made you use the shotgun. I should have given you a rifle or even a bigger handgun. It was my fault, not yours."

"I don't care whose fault it was."

"Larry, I swear, if there's any shooting to be done, I'll do it. Or I'll call on Byron or Plaskowitz or some other halfwit." Tull stopped, stared into the distance, picturing the consequences, shook his head. "God help me," he murmured, "I'll see that you aren't the one responsible. Plaskowitz..." He shook his head again, a mournful expression on his face. "I just hope no one gets hurt," he whispered.

"Oh, man!" Tull had scored a hit. Larry Kalmakoff had a very tender sense of responsibility and Jim Tull, that conniving bastard, had just tweaked it. "That would be a disaster!"

"Great! I knew we could count on you, Larry." Tull brightened, all smiles now.

"Hey! Hold on! I'm quitting, I said…"

"And the town appreciates it, too, or would if it had any brains, which is an open question." Tull rooted in his desk drawer for a cigar.

"No! I can't, Jim, I just can't!"

"Now here's the schedule I've drawn up. You see that you only have to work eight days running and one of those is a half-day, only eight hours." Tull clamped his teeth on a rum crook and fired it up.

"Lord, no! That's…"

"This year we'll have around eighty volunteers working security…"

"What!" Larry was horrified. "That's twice as many as last year!"

"Yes. Wonderful to see town spirit like that, isn't it?"

"But you know they cause more trouble than they do anything else." Arcadia was less than six thousand population and had a tiny police force, the smallest in Canada, maybe, or at any rate British Columbia's smallest, with four officers and one civilian employee. LakeFest would draw at least twenty-five thousand visitors, maybe more, over the five days. City Council didn't want to spend hard-earned festival dollars on an outside security firm, so a force was drawn from local volunteers. The fact that these volunteers ranged from power-happy gun freaks to partying boozers meant that they needed as much policing as the festival-goers. "Jim, this will be a disaster!"

"Oh, now, Larry, you're just being pessimistic. I'm sure that, with a little guidance, this will be a credible security force."

"Wait a minute!" Larry knew he was beaten. "No guns! All right?" Larry waved away the smoke clouding Tull's head and pointed a finger in his face. "You arm any of them, just one, goddammit! And I quit! I'll throw my badge on the ground and walk away."

"Well, Larry…"

"No! That's final!"

"Well, I was going to say, this year, no guns. Just like you want, Larry." Tull shook his head. "Doug Blaney really will not be happy. He may not be part of security this year."

"Good! He's a nutcase! One of these days we'll have a homicide and Blaney is my number one suspect right away."

"Oh, now, Doug's not that bad."

"Last year he wanted to tear gas the audience!"

"Well, but we didn't allow that, did we?"

"Remember when he pistol-whipped that tourist?"

"Larry, that was years ago! We've all learned a lot about running a festival since then." Tull sucked on his cigar. "Anyway, the guy was creating a disturbance."

"He booed a musician, Jim. I felt like booing myself." The musician was a country singer from the States who had a song about the craven French and Canadian cowards who wouldn't join righteous Americans in the invasion of Iraq. Blaney's view was that Iraq should not only be invaded, but totally destroyed, in order to teach people not to have Saddams in charge.

"Those were tense days, Larry, but it's all water under the bridge now."

"Yeah, not even Blaney wants us over there anymore. He just wants to nuke Iran."

"Now, let's not get into politics, Larry." Tull blew out a stream of smoke. "So this year the security forces will be equipped with batons."

"Oh God, no!"

"These are special batons, Larry, turned out of fine mill-ends by local craftsmen."

Larry understood. "You mean somebody's formed a company to make sticks and the Festival Committee is going to buy them."

"Exactly!" Tull smiled. "I couldn't put it better myself."

"And let me guess, the company belongs to members of the Committee board or Council members, right?"

"Now we can't have board members profiting from contracts let by the Committee, that would be a conflict of interest. No, the Fest-a-Rod company is owned by two town councillors, Jerry Stoneman and Pete Rimbert."

But Stoneman's brother is on the Committee and so is Rimbert's wife."

Tull shrugged. "It's a small town, Larry."

2

Not only was Arcadia a small town, it was getting smaller every day. In 1999, when the mill closed, Arcadia had a population of more than fourteen thousand. Now it was about fifty-eight hundred and shrinking. Unable to keep up their mortgages, unemployed millworkers had walked away from them. The south end of town had whole blocks of empty houses all in the process of foreclosure. LakeFest was the only industry the town had left. Since 2001, the town had hosted the music festival that originally had lasted two days and now went on for five days. City Council wanted it to be even longer since the LakeFest earnings had to last Arcadia for the rest of the year.

Larry understood all that, knew that the town depended on LakeFest, but still he hated it. Heatstroke, puking children, belligerent drunks, the "business community" demanding that he both keep order and not bother Festival attendees. Every year something bad happened. Every year the Festival got bigger. Every year the bad things got worse. Then, last year, the worst so far: the bear.

Festival performances were held at the far end of town in a huge area between the highway and the lake that had been cleared of forest. Once, there had been a plan to build a mall there, but that died with the mill. The stage was set up just above the beach. That afternoon, a bluegrass group was jangling away when Larry spotted the bear, a yearling black, fat and stupid. It had gotten past the fence somehow and ambled onto the beach. Now it stood there swaying its head from the beach to the crowd, trying to find a way out.

Larry grabbed his radio, trying to raise Tull, and made his way forward. People in the crowd began noticing the bear. Parents pointed it out to children and some of them started walking toward the beach. "No," Larry yelled, "Stay back!"

Larry pushed forward to the crowd's edge and tried to wave people away. The bear started for the area back of the stage where the bands had their Winnebagoes and equipment trailers. Larry unsnapped his holster and grabbed his weapon. Jim Tull caught up to him and thrust a shotgun in his hand. "Don't take a chance with this crowd! Use the shotgun!"

Larry nodded and moved forward. He pumped a round into the chamber and ran between the bear and the stage. The bear saw him, stopped, and began moving back toward the crowd. People were streaming toward the beach, laughing, holding their kids up high to see the bear. The animal stopped, frightened now, and made a low moaning sound. It turned and rushed toward the lake, then back toward the fence. People kept coming.

When Larry caught up to the bear, the crowd was less than twenty meters away. "Stay back!" He screamed at the crowd but there was no stopping the flow of people. The bear turned and faced Larry, showing its teeth. A string of slobber hung from its muzzle and its eyes rolled in fear, flashing white. The bear gathered itself to charge and Larry raised the shotgun and fired.

The load caught the bear in the shoulder and face. The bear screamed and rose onto its hind legs but the load of number four shot was too light to bring it down. Larry fired again, right into the bear's upright torso. The bear dropped and made for the lake, stepping in its own guts. Larry ran after it. The bear thrashed in the foaming red water. This time, Larry drew his handgun, waded in, and got as close to the frantic bear as he could. He put a shot right behind the bear's ear and it quit bellowing. The only sound was the bluegrass music still plinkety-planking from the stage when Larry raised his weapon and fired a second shot into the animal, just to be sure.

The bear's carcass lay in the shallows, intestines billowing in the red water. Children began screaming and crying. Larry turned around to see hundreds of horrified faces staring into his. He sloshed out of the lake and along the beach, past the crowd. All along the way, parents pulled their children close, protecting them, keeping them safe from Larry the monster.

It was all still there, the frightened children, the bear's agony, the screams, that damned bluegrass music…"I don't know if I can do this, Jim."

"Arcadia needs you, Larry. Without you, it's screwed. The town would be destroyed, just a smoking ruin by the lake." Tull pulled at his cigar. He seemed cheerful enough as he contemplated the picture.

3

Larry thought about Arcadia as an abandoned ruin as he cruised the neighbourhood above the mill. Named Dogwood Park by the developers, people called it Dogpatch now. Three of every four houses were abandoned and paint was peeling even on the places with occupants. No one could afford to keep their place in repair. Down the slope, across the highway, the mill that was once the town's reason for being disintegrated behind steel mesh fences topped with razor wire. In the early days, logs were rafted right up to the mill but the lake boats were all gone now. The railroad that used to run past town had been torn out and not even a bicycle trail was left. Only the highway remained to tie Arcadia to the rest of the world.

Across the lake, the forest spread down the mountains to the narrow beach. High above, where the green trees ended, ragged peaks and bright white patches of glacier framed the sky. Arcadia was at the bottom of a bowl; you could turn around in a circle, eyes following the rim, grow dizzy, feel the weight of the ice and rocks and trees hanging above the lake. It was beautiful. Larry felt the beauty swell his heart, but it was frightening, too, to live small and fragile beneath that hanging mass.

Larry caught a furtive motion behind the window of a house that should be empty. He pulled into the drive and walked up the front steps. He remembered the family that had lived here, the Gilkers, gone now for several years. The front door was locked. Larry walked down the steps and started around the back, his heels clattering on the sidewalk. He stopped, listened for a moment, then quietly moved back to the front. The kids were just running out onto the porch when he got there.

"Okay, just hold it." The boys froze. There were three of them, eleven or twelve year-olds, Larry judged. One of them was Balbir Singh. Larry walked up the steps. "You fellows do any damage?" He herded them back into the house.

There was an old sofa left in the living room. Larry made a mental note, had to get rid of that before older youths started bringing girls here. The smell of cigarette smoke hung in the air. These boys had been tasting a different forbidden fruit. "So, let me have the stuff." The boys looked at each other, pretending not to know what Larry wanted. "Don't make me search you guys, okay?"

"I want a lawyer." It was Balbir talking. Of all of them, it would have to be him.

"You get legal advice later, after you're arrested, taken down to the station, fingerprinted, and charged." Larry leaned on the last word, trying to make it sound like something physical that might cause pain. "Right now, I search you and take the contraband." One of the boys, a Talbot, Larry guessed, looked down at the floor, then pulled a pack of cigarettes from inside his shirt. "Lighter, too." Larry took the cigarettes from the Talbot boy and looked at the other two. He was more interested in getting the lighter from them than the cigarettes. Larry could imagine a fire starting with a butt dropped in that couch, catching, then sweeping through Dogpatch. The inadequate volunteer fire department response, the families still living here trapped in the inferno...

"Come on, now, who has it?" The other two boys carefully didn't look at Balbir, who crossed his arms and stared straight into Larry's eyes. Larry could see the lighter's outline in Balbir's jeans pocket. "Come on, Balbir, hand it over."

The two stared at each other for a minute, then the boy dropped his gaze and pulled the lighter out. "No law against having this," he said.

"You sure about that? Abandoned house like this, serious fire hazard? Why, possessing arson tools on top of breaking and entering…" Larry shook his head. "Pretty serious."

"We weren't going to burn anything! Really!" One of the other boys piped up. He was scared. Balbir was still defiant.

Larry didn't respond. He went over to the sofa and pulled up the cushions, running his hand down behind the springs. No cigarette butts. "Where's your ashtray?" One of the boys pointed out a jar lid in the corner. Larry made sure there were no live butts inside, then toured the house. The kitchen door was ajar. Larry tested the lock. Broken. He pulled the screen shut and hooked it. That would have to do for the time being. He wrote the house number down in his notebook. Have to find out if the bank owns it yet. If so, they needed to look after it.

"All right, you boys, this is pretty bad. Can you imagine how awful it would be if one of these houses caught fire?"

"We didn't start any fire."

"But you could have, right? Accident or not, that would be terrible, people hurt, burned to death in their houses…" Larry let it sink in. "Well, it would cause your parents a lot of grief if they found out what you were up to." A little gleam of hope flickered behind the eyes of two of the boys, but not Balbir. "So I want you to promise me, I want your solemn word, that you won't break into any more of these houses." Two of the boys were already nodding. Balbir crossed his arms and stared into Larry's eyes. "So if I catch you again, it will go twice as hard on you because not only will you be committing a crime, you'll be breaking your word!" He paused. "Don't go giving your word if you're going to break it! You're better off just being arrested and charged. Now, do I have your word?" Larry asked each boy in turn. For a moment he was afraid Balbir would challenge him, but the boy gave in and made a sullen promise. "Okay, then. Go on home now."

Larry made certain the front door was locked. He watched the boys walking down the street, arms waving as they talked to each other about what had just happened. There you go, he thought, another fine piece of police work. Lord, he thought, I really should quit. To hell with Tull, to hell with this town, let it burn! Then he caught a flash of red across the lake that flickered along the rippled water. The last glow of the sun as it set edged the grey peaks with a red corona and turned the glacier ice pink. The entire panorama was reflected in the lake for whole minutes as Larry stood there, enthralled by the spectacle, then the sun dropped a little lower and the mountains turned dark and the lake lost their image. Lights were coming on in town. Here and there they reflected from the water, tiny points against the darkness. Larry sighed and got back in his car. He had to finish his patrol duties before he could go down to the station and clock out.

4

Breakfast at the Victory Café was Larry's high point of the day. It wasn't that the eggs were any better than anyplace else, but the waitress was something special. When Anusheela would smile, taking Larry's order, well, her smile just brightened his whole life, for a while anyway. Anusheela's husband, Jogwinder, had left her and their son, Balbir, when the mill closed. He was there one day and gone the next, no one knew where. Larry thought Jogwinder was a complete fool.

Anusheela was serving another booth when she looked up and spotted Larry. She didn't smile; her face pulled into a worried frown. Uh oh, thought Larry, must be about Balbir the day before. Larry ran the incident through his mind. He thought he'd handled it okay. Probably Anusheela just wanted some reassurance that her son wasn't turning into a career criminal or something. Larry didn't mind reassuring her, was looking forward to it, in fact, when Bob Weber slid his chunky body into the seat opposite. Bob was just about the last person Larry wanted to see.

"Larry, I want to talk to you."

"Oh?"

"Yeah. Hold on a minute while I tell this pretty lady what I want." Anusheela didn't react, just took Weber's order. Larry tried to catch her eye but she kept her gaze on her order pad. He asked for the usual: eggs over easy, sausages, coffee.

"Brown toast?"

"Yes, please, Anusheela." He hadn't said on purpose, wanted to hear her speak. Of course she knew his order, she'd been serving him the same breakfast every working morning for two years. She walked off without even a glance toward him. Larry thought about finding a way to speak to her in private. He was cautious about being alone with her or any other single woman. It was too easy for rumours to get started in this town. Larry became aware that Weber was prattling on about the upcoming meeting.

Weber was saying, "Arcadia needs LakeFest. The business community thinks…"

Larry shuddered -- the words "the business community" always made him shudder – and he winced – hearing Bob Weber pretend to be a businessman always made him wince. "Bob, I'll be there. You know I will."

"That's great, Larry. You know we all have difficulties in this life, things that we have to get past…"

Larry tuned him out, the way he always did when Bob started reciting a sermon from an Amway flyer. Or Melaleuca. Or whatever he was selling this month. Difficulties! What the hell did Bob know about difficulties, did he wake up sweating from a dream full of screams and blood and crying children? Maybe, thought Larry, I should just turn in my badge and my gun and go sell jojoba or tea tree oil or whatever Bob was peddling now. "What are you selling now, Bob?"

Weber stalled in the middle of a sentence, adjusting his brain to the question. Larry thought he could hear gears grinding, wondered if Bob's eyes would start spinning. "Larry," said Bob quietly, "Larry, have you ever heard of the Tahitian noni fruit?"

"Noni fruit."

"That's right! Clinical trials show that noni juice will shrink tumours in mice." Weber nodded so hard that his jowls shook. He looked a little like a tropical fruit, thought Larry.

"Shrinks mouse tumours."

"That's right. Cigarette smokers who have…"

"Bob, weren't you selling mangosteen juice last month?"

"That's right, Larry, but now I…"

"'The Queen of Tropical Fruits', you said."

"Well, yes, but noni is superior to mangosteen. I'm not saying mangosteen isn't good, but noni is superior in every way. You know why noni is superior, Larry?"

"No, Bob, tell me why noni is superior to mangosteen."

"Larry," Bob leaned in, "the noni fruit is superior because it has A Unique Heritage." Bob sat back and nodded. "Yessir, the noni fruit has *a unique heritage*."

"Okay, Bob. Well, I don't have cancer or…" Bob started to say something. "Or any other health issues, so I'll just pass on the noni fruit, okay?"

"Okay, Larry. Say, I've still got my mangosteen sales kit. I could let you have it, samples and all, at a substantial discount."

"That's fine, Bob, but I have a job. I can't just quit and go out selling mangosteens."

"Actually, Larry, I thought you were quitting."

"Why'd you think that?"

"Just something I picked up..."

Larry hadn't told anyone of his plans and Jim Tull wouldn't have mentioned yesterday's meeting. But Weber had worked it out. How could a guy that knows so much about people be such a rotten salesman? "No, Bob, I'm not quitting. I'll be there at LakeFest. Unless people want to call in my contract, of course." I can only hope, Larry thought.

"Oh, no, Larry! No way that's going to happen. That's why I came to talk to you, to let you know how the business community feels." Larry shuddered. "You have our full confidence, Larry, and, barring any further problems of course, we're right behind you."

"Of course." Larry thought about sticking his badge where Bob would feel it every time he sat down.

Doug Blaney dropped into the seat beside Weber. "So what the hell is this thing about sticks?" No preamble, just right in your face, Blaney was all about attack.

"I don't have the details yet, Doug'" said Larry. "I'll know more after today's meeting." Anusheela set down his breakfast on the table. Larry tried to catch her eye but she turned to Blaney and took his order for coffee.

"Well, I think it's a hell of a thing. How you going to stop a biker gang with sticks is what I want to know. You need firepower." Blaney pulled a paper from his shirt pocket and unfolded it on the table. "Look: twenty to thirty volunteer officers armed with good handguns working the crowd. I recommend Glocks. Then three quick reaction strike units of eight to ten men, one each side, north, south, east. These men should be armed with riot guns, double O for the first three shells, rest of the magazine loaded with slugs." Blaney raised his head from the plan he had drawn up. "None of those pissant duck loads like you got stuck with last year. You need slugs for bear, or double ought, anyway." He paused. Larry kept his head down, shovelled eggs into his mouth. "All right, then on platforms mounted on the sound towers beside the stage you put the heavy stuff." Heavy stuff? Larry thought, My God! "I think a couple of .30 calibre automatic rifles and one .50." Blaney stopped and held up a hand. "Now I know that some would say we need two, at least, of the .50s, but think about it, with three automatic weapons on the towers and the pump guns along the perimeter, we can clean out everything on the Festival grounds."

Weber was interested. "Suppose they break through the guys with riot guns?"

"I've said right from the time people started talking Festival years ago: razor wire and lots of it. Kept your crowd controlled and you can control the crowd."

"And the guards with handguns, the ones in with the crowd? What happens to them when the machine guns open up?"

"I have to go check in at the station. Got that meeting after," Larry mumbled through a mouthful of toast. Larry walked away as Blaney explained the difference between friendly fire and collateral damage to Weber.

Anusheela was behind the cash register. "Nan, what's wrong?"

"What happened with Balbir yesterday?"

"He and some other boys were involved in a little mischief, that's all. They got inside an empty house in Dogpatch and…"

"So why did you threaten to arrest him?"

"Uh…"

"Did you point a gun at him?"

"Oh, no, Nan. In fact I left my weapon in the car." Larry wasn't wearing a gun. He usually left his gun belt in the lock box between the front seats.

"Did you have to frighten him that way?" Anusheela's eyes blazed.

"Nan, I'm just trying to stop this from becoming a serious problem. If there was a fire…"

"You should have called me! I will deal with Balbir! Me!"

Larry glimpsed Blaney and Weber rising from the booth and bearing down on him. "Nan, can we talk about this? Later, I mean. Privately."

Anusheela lifted her chin in the air. "Here is your change. <u>Sir!</u>" That last word burned a hole right through Larry's chest.

5

Larry had to stop by the station. He had told Weber and Blaney he was going to check in and he didn't want to make himself a liar. Fran Doucet sat behind the front desk, reading a tabloid. "You got a meeting, don't forget."

"I wish I could," said Larry.

"What's the matter? You coming down with something? I heard there was flu going around."

"No, I feel good, Fran, just fine."

"You don't look it. You miss breakfast this morning?"

"No, I just came from the Victory."

"Usually, you have breakfast, you look a lot more perky. Anusheela not there?"

"No, she was there. We spoke. Her son got in a little mischief yesterday."

Fran stared at him over her spectacles, waiting. "I caught him and some other kids in an empty house in Dogpatch, gave them a stern warning, you know?"

Fran sat silent as a judge, holding her tabloid in both hands, waiting.

"Anusheela thinks I was too hard on the kid, scared him, she says. Fran, I swear I…"

"That woman is upset because she thinks she's losing control over her son. It can be hard on mothers when boys get that age. But what she needs is a man in her life, not to control her son, but to make her feel better about parenting. You go see her, talk to her about Balbir."

"Well, I don't know…"

"Doesn't matter what you say, just tell her she's doing a good job and that she's not a complete washout as a mother. Understand?"

"Fran, I…"

"Just do it, Larry. My God, how long has her husband been gone?"

"About five years, six…"

"Too soon to declare the bastard dead, I guess. Go talk to her. Jesus!" Fran shook her head, raised the newspaper back to her eyes. Larry hoped that she was through with the lecture. He felt like a second-grader explaining to the teacher how the dog ate his homework.

"Uh, check out this place with the bank," He handed Fran the address of the abandoned Gilker house. "See if they own it yet or who's responsible for it."

"Sure. Now hurry up," Fran said, not taking her eyes from her paper. "Meeting's about to start."

Yes'm, thought Larry, but he knew better than to make a wiseass remark. Anyway, maybe he should go see Anusheela and get this thing straightened out.

Fran glanced up and shook her head as Larry walked out the door. Stupid man! The older she got, the more she wondered how the silly human race managed to keep on reproducing. She went back to reading her tabloid.

6

Mayor Ed Wolichuk called the meeting to order. "Okay, we're in the countdown to LakeFest now, only a few weeks left, and it's time to tighten up the hanging threads. Now, first item we need to discuss is security. Of course, the police are ready, right, Jim?"

"Right as rain, your Worship," said Tull.

"That's good, then. We know we can count on you. Now we also have the volunteer security force. This year, as you know, we'll be giving batons to the top wage tier." People serving as Festival security were paid varying amounts. All the volunteers at LakeFest were paid something.

Jim Tull said, "Now, your Worship, I need to ask, what kind of training will people be getting about these bats?"

"Fest-A-Rods," snarled Janet Rimbert, "We call them Fest-A-Rods." Janet represented the Festival Committee.

Pete Rimbert, councilman and Janet's husband, leaned across the table, "This could be something we can market after our Festival is over." He drew a breath. "There might be *jobs* in this," he intoned. Jobs! Everyone was silent for a moment at hearing the magic word.

Mayor Wolichuk broke the spell, "It's these little seeds that sprout mighty oaks."

"Let's hope so," said Tull, "Because eventually we'll run out of mill ends and then we'll need something else to carve into, ah, rods. But, anyway, about that training…"

"Yes," said the Mayor, "Of course we want to make certain our volunteers can use the Fest-A-Rods properly."

Councillor Jerry Stoneman took charge, "You have to understand, Jim, that a major function of the

Fest-A-Rod is deterrence. Would-be troublemakers see security personnel carrying these batons and they think twice about creating a problem."

Wolichuk said, "Carry a big stick and you don't need to speak."

Tull nodded. "I get it. But suppose someone does cause trouble. How will security respond?"

"Jim, we've got an expert right here in Arcadia who has volunteered to handle training."

"An expert what? Stick-handler?"

"No, no, Jim," chuckled the Mayor, "We've got plenty of fine hockey players," He gestured toward Jack and Jerry Stoneman, once local athletic stars, "But now you've got the bark off the wrong tree."

"We figured the local police wouldn't be able to handle this," Pete Rimbert glared at Tull, "So we found somebody who could." Rimbert, like most of Council, hated Jim Tull.

"Well, you're right there, Pete," said Tull. "I just wouldn't know where to begin telling someone how to use a Fest-A-Rod. No, I haven't even seen one. It's a mystery to me." He grinned at Rimbert.

"Here's one," Janet Rimbert picked up a stick from the floor and whacked the table hard. Everyone except Jim Tull jumped.

"Well, that's a handy piece of timber," said Tull. "Mind if I look at it? My, my. I like the way the ends are rounded off, good craftsmanship there. And it feels just right, too." He handed it to Larry.

The Fest-A-Rod was a smooth piece of wood over two feet long and maybe an inch and a half or so in diameter. Some writing was stamped on one end. Fest-A-Rod Enterprises, Arcadia, BC, Canada. And a little maple leaf. "That's for export," said Jack Stoneman, "The maple leaf is required."

"Patent pending?"

"Crane Baxter is looking into that for us." Baxter was a lawyer who represented the city.

"And this says, uh, 'Proverbs 26:3'. Is that 'Spare the rod…'?"

"No, it's 'A bridle for horses, a whip for mules, a rod for the back of fools.'" Pete Rimbert leaned hard on the last word as he looked directly at Tull.

"Actually," Janet corrected her husband, "It's the whip for a horse, the bridle for a mule…"

"Whatever. You get the idea." Pete and Janet Rimbert were members of The Fountain of Blood Church, an evangelical congregation.

"Hmm," said Tull, "I wonder how Festival attendees will like being called fools." A look of alarm passed across Mayor Wolichuk's face. "Perhaps a reference to the 23rd psalm would be better. You know, about thy rod comforting me and so on. I know I'm comforted just seeing this instrument."

"We'll think about it," grated Rimbert.

"Maybe, if public money is behind this, we should be more secular," David Cantor suggested. Cantor was a young lawyer who mostly worked Legal Aid cases. He was the token progressive on Council. Cantor had a well-developed sense of justice that sometimes clashed with Larry's own notions. The two hadn't actually quarrelled yet, but Larry was careful around him.

"This is private enterprise," snapped Rimbert, "Creating tax-paying jobs, the kind that support government programs." Like Legal Aid, he didn't say.

"Perhaps so," said Cantor, "But you're offering support right here…"

"The Committee is an independent body…" began Janet Rimbert.

"The Committee has earned our support!" Pete yelled over his wife.

"But we are not all Christians and perhaps the Bible verse needs re-thinking."

"Yes," said Wolichuk, stepping in to make the peace, "That might be a good idea. To re-think this. Sleep on it and see if we feel any new angles." The Rimberts sat red-faced and frowning, but stifled their anger. "Anyway, back to your question, Jim, about training." The Mayor paused dramatically, "We have looked within and found local talent."

"Do tell," said Tull.

"Yes," said Wolichuk. He took a breath, then announced, "Dolphin Starlight will handle the training." Larry was dumbfounded. Dolphin Starlight was a hippy entrepreneur. Larry thought he was an airhead. Actually, Larry thought all hippies were airheads. "Dolphin is a tai chi expert, of course," said the Mayor, "and, you may not be aware, but combat with a staff is part of tai chi."

"Combat with a staff? Isn't the guy a pacifist?"

"Now I didn't ask about his politics, Larry, but I did look into the tai chi part of things and it looks just about perfect for the sort of peace-keeping we want our volunteers to accomplish."

Pete Rimbert snarled at Larry, "Aren't *you* a pacifist? I thought you were Russian. Isn't Kalmakoff a Russian name?"

Larry sat stunned. He was a Doukhobor, or at least his parents had been. The Doukhobors were pacifist Russians who immigrated to Canada in the Nineteenth Century, after refusing the Czar's military service and burning their weapons. Their subsequent history in British Columbia was very troubled. Larry always choked when someone brought up his background.

"Well, now, Christians are pacifists, too," Tull broke in, "At least so I've heard. But that doesn't stop them from using the rod, now does it?"

"He doesn't even carry a gun most of the time!"

Tull swished the Fest--A-Rod in the air. "Different strokes for different folks. Right, Your Worship?"

"Certainly," said Wolichuk, "And, I think this year, our best-laid plan is this different one."

Tull was grinning. "Well, that sounds fine to me. Actually, I'd rather have weapons in the hands of pacifists, less danger of anyone getting hurt."

"Um, yes," Wolichuk couldn't decide what to say to that. "So if that's all settled, we can move along to the next order of affairs. Jim, you have that police schedule?"

"Right here, Your Worship. I'm afraid there's a fair amount of overtime." Pete Rimbert said something under his breath. Tull turned toward him. "The force can just work regular hours, of course, if you don't want to authorize the overtime pay. I'm sure Dolphin Starlight and his crew can handle things just fine while we're away."

"Now, Jim, I'm certain Council will go along with your recommendations. We'll discuss it with full Council present. In camera, of course."

"Of course."

"Now there's just one thing, Jim, based on our experience here in the past." Wolichuk paused. Oh no, thought Larry, don't say it. But Wolichuk went on,

"Maybe pay some extra consideration to animal control this year, Jim. Okay?" No one looked at Larry.

"Why, certainly, Your Worship," Tull grinned, "This year we'll be loaded for bear."

Lord! Larry thought.

7

Outside the meeting room, Larry said, "Thanks for watching my back in there. You know, about the Russian thing." He had to admit that Jim Tull always looked out for his people.

"No problem, Larry." Tull gestured toward his squad car. "What say we drive out to Mr. Starshine's place and see what he has in mind?"

"I still don't understand how martial arts can be used without hurting someone."

"Well, Grasshopper, you need to trust the Force."

"The Force?"

"Or whatever these tai cheese worship."

"Right. I think chi is breath or something."

"There you are: all air. How can someone be hurt by… Unless the air is a big wind, blows down all the trees. But then you could see the forest, right?"

"You always do this after you talk to Wolichuk."

"Now, Grasshopper, suppose a rod was spared in the forest but no tai cheese were around, would it make a sound?"

"Jim? Stop. Okay?"

Dolphin Starlight lived up the mountain on the edge of town. About twenty years back, he bought a cheap piece of land and set up a teepee. He wasn't called Dolphin yet, that came after he formed the commune. The commune's purpose was for members to discover inner spirituality through natural living. Everyone in the group took new names. They built Dolphin's log house, a big four-room place, but slept outside in teepees right through the winter, being closer to nature that way. Some members developed pneumonia and one lost some frostbitten toes. Dolphin and certain female communards slept indoors. Larry imagined there was quite a bit of competition among the young women members of the commune for the privilege of being chosen to stay warm through the winter. Eventually the commune members drifted away, back to the city or their parents, some back to their old names, some keeping the new ones. Now Dolphin held workshops and spiritual gatherings. People from all over came and paid to sleep in the teepees and attend these sessions. Dolphin Starlight was a gainfully employed hippy and gainful employment made him a man of standing in the community.

Twenty or so people were grouped in the grassy meadow just below Dolphin's cabin. Dolphin stood before them wearing loose black robes, making grand sweeping movements with a Fest-a-Rod. Everyone dutifully imitated Dolphin's moves. "Hyaa! Wah! Ha!" yelled Dolphin. "Yai! Waa! Hunh!" echoed the group as they slashed and advanced across the meadow. Larry thought of crowd control tactics he had seen demonstrated in police training sessions. Not many mobs in Arcadia, but a group like this could cause trouble. Larry saw himself, a lone cop, as a rank of his neighbours advanced on him with sticks. "Hai!" Larry shuddered.

"Isn't that Mildred Blaney out front? Doug's wife?"

"Yep," agreed Tull, "Going to combat school. Look out, Doug!"

"I wish!" Larry had been called to the Blaneys' house many times by neighbours who had heard a racket. Not that Mildred ever yelled or screamed or even cried, she was always quiet as she stood there bleeding, eye beginning to swell, and lied about falling down the stairs or running into a door. Never once had she filed a complaint against her husband. "Be nice to see her stand up for herself."

"Probably never happen. Pretty impressive group, though, don't you think? I bet they'd scare the pants off the Hell's Angels."

Larry took in the crowd of earnest housewives and skinny hippies. "Sure," he said. "They scare me."

"That's the spirit! Bolster their confidence! Looks like they'll be a while. Let's go talk to Yoda."

Dolphin Starlight saw them coming and called one of the group to the front to take over. "Just keep them doing the same three moves, Connie. Hit the Snake, Open the Door, Snap the Branch. The sequence should flow naturally, without thought, advancing all the while." He dropped the rod on his shoulder, like a soldier's rifle, and marched over. "Officers! Come to see our progress?"

"They gonna break bones with those chakras?"

Starlight's features writhed in confusion before settling into an expression of benign amusement. "Chakras?"

"Isn't that what you call these sticks? Like those ones attached by a chain?" Tull was into his yokel act now.

"Oh! You mean nunchuks."

"Yeah, chucks, chaks, something like that."

"Actually, this is called cane form."

"Oh, yeah? Cane, eh? So what you have them doing is breaking snakes?"

"Hit the Snake. It's the name of the move. The idea is to stop someone with a weapon, a gun or knife, even a bottle."

"Uh-huh."

"So the first move strikes the wrist, hopefully making the subject drop the weapon. Whether he does or not, the next move is Open the Door, a direct strike to the midsection, then recovery with Snap the Branch."

"Rinse and repeat."

"If necessary," Starlight agreed. "So what do you think? Effective?"

"Looks that way to me. But how do you handle an unarmed drunk? Don't want to Open *His* Door, he might puke all over you."

"Everyone will have the usual training in communication dynamics, same as last year. We are all aware of the public relations issues."

"Well, last year a volunteer got a little too dynamic with a young woman. She claimed he grabbed her tit and the city lawyer had to use all his communication skills to avoid a lawsuit."

Dolphin Starlight smiled softly. "I don't believe that person will be part of the security arrangements this year. In fact, I think he's left town. These things happen, Jim, we do the best we can."

"Wisdom of the East?"

"Here in the West, we say: Speak softly and carry a big stick."

"You know the mayor said something very similar to me just a little while ago."

"Ah. I'm certain it was similar."

"Great minds think alike, I guess."

"There are many wells of wisdom, but we all drink the same water."

Neither Starlight or Tull actually broke out laughing. They just stood there smiling, nodding at each. These two understand each other pretty well, thought Larry.

On the walk back to the car Larry asked, "Why do you play such a fool when you talk to him? Like some kind of ignorant hayseed?"

"Oh, it seems to bring out the best in Mister Starlight when you let him educate you."

"And you play a different role when you talk to Council. You act different with everyone."

"That way everyone understands me."

"I try to be the same with everyone."

"That's why they all see you differently, Larry." Tull stopped and looked directly at him. "But don't try to change. You're an honest man, Larry, you try to play-act, people will think you're a phony."

"Wisdom of the West?"

"Straight talk, Amigo. Now let's head back to town. Sit around and contemplate the low crime rate, enjoy this quiet time before the tourists start arriving."

8

Anusheela worked from seven to two, six days a week. During LakeFest she would put in extra hours during the evening dinner rush. She wouldn't get overtime; ignoring the Labour Code was part of the price of having a full-time job in Arcadia. Anyway, the tourists tipped a lot better than the townspeople, so Anusheela would do well enough. At 1:55, Larry parked behind the Victory and waited for her to get off work. At 2:05 she walked out the back, uniform rolled up under one arm, tossed a bag of trash into the dumpster, and started down the alley.

"Nan!"

Anusheela whirled around to face the vehicle, hands on her hips, eyebrows drawing together and forming a hard vertical line above her nose. Larry was scared to death as he walked up to her. "Going to arrest me?" she spat.

"Oh, Nan… Look, Balbir wasn't doing anything all that wrong…"

"But *you* had to frighten him anyway, didn't you, Mister High-and-Mighty Policeman?"

"He wasn't that frightened. "I…"

"Oh? Isn't that too bad! Maybe you should have taken him to the police station, shined a light in his eyes, beat him with a stick!"

The Fest-A-Rod popped into Larry's consciousness and he suppressed it. "No. Nan, he's not a bad kid…"

"Bad enough to have to be threatened by armed thugs."

Larry didn't say, No threats, I wasn't armed, but moved right into his agenda: "You're doing a good job with that boy, Nan." She paused for a moment, listening. Thank you, Fran! "And he's a good kid. All those empty houses are just a problem waiting to happen."

"So why don't you do something about them!"

"I would if I could. So I got him to promise me he wouldn't go back in them, that's all."

"Promise?"

"I made him give me his solemn word."

Nan thought a minute, nodded. "Man-to-man stuff, eh?"

"Sort of like that…" Larry was cautious, not certain what was going to follow.

"Yes," said Anusheela, "He needs a man to talk to him. It is so hard…" She shook her head and Larry was suddenly afraid she was going to cry.

"Nan, you're doing a great job raising him. And he's a great kid, really. But every boy gets into a little mischief. It's curiosity mostly, all those houses to explore."

"Yes, you see? You know these things. What can a woman know? And there is rebellion, I can see it coming. When parents are mixed then there is trouble, my mother tried to tell me."

"Mixed?" Larry was confused. He thought Jogwinder and Anusheela were both from India. Or Pakistan. Or one of those.

"Jogwinder was Sikh, I am Hindu. It is why Balbir has a mixed name. He is also Singh, you see." She looked up at Larry.

"Oh, sure, I see." He nodded, not having a clue what she was talking about.

"So now he wants to be neither. He wants to be Canadian. He wants to eat Canadian food. Not masala and vegetables, he says. No! He wants spaghetti and roast beef like Canadians eat."

"Well…"

"I give him hamburgers, okay. I give him beef, now he wants pork! Pork! Like the Chinese!"

"Uh…"

"I don't know what to do."

"You're doing fine, Nan!" Stick to the theme. "And these, uh, food issues will straighten out."

"You think so?" Anusheela looked directly at Larry with the biggest, most trusting eyes he had ever seen.

"Nan, when he gets older he's going to remember all these dishes as home. He's going to eat, uh, masala and think of you."

"Really?"

"Yes. I think you're doing great, Nan, just great!" Larry wished he could think of something else to say besides "great".

Anusheela smiled at him. "You see? You understand these things."

"Well, Balbir's grandparents…"

"Pah! I have not spoken to my family since I ran off with Jogwinder. Let them think I am dead!"

Burned your bridges, thought Larry. You really are all alone, aren't you? "Nan, I bet they pray you aren't."

"I don't care. I will never give them the satisfaction of knowing I am alive." Anusheela's lips clamped together.

Okay. End this topic right now. "You're doing a good job with Balbir." I wish to hell I could find another way to say that, Larry thought, I sound like a complete idiot.

"Still, he needs a man to talk to him about man things. Boys do." She paused. "Do you think..?"

"Anything I can do, Nan, just say the word. I mean, I can talk to him but…"

"But it is no good when you are all in uniform on the job and all, isn't that so?"

"Oh. Yes. Right."

"I tell you what, you come over to my house for supper some time, get to know Balbir."

"Oh, okay. I mean, yes! Great! I'd love to."

"All right. Sunday. Five o'clock."

"Fine. Great! Uh, we'll have masala, right?"

"We'll have biryani. It has masala in it."

"Sounds good! Can I bring anything? A bottle of wine?" Do Hindus drink? Do Sikhs? Is this like Muslims?

"Some beer, maybe."

"Great! I'll be there!"

There were places in the world, Larry knew, that had very fast internet. Arcadia wasn't one of them. There were no cell towers in a hundred miles and lots of mountains all around, so no cell phones, as well as no wireless. The LakeFest committee pitched this to tourists as a feature: "Escape Gadget Dependence And Free Your Soul!" There was talk about financing a leaflet that linked cell phones to brain cancer, but the committee decided that it cost too much. Let the tourists do their own research.

Not only did the town lack broadband but available dial-up speed came nowhere close to 28k, the standard slowest speed in most parts of the country. Larry grew twitchy as he waited for a page to form on the library monitor. Come on, he silently urged the computer, I want to see Wikipedia in action. Then he thought, the hell with it, I'll use the encyclopedia while I'm waiting. He took down the Britannica S volume from the shelf and turned to the article on Sikhs. He had almost finished it when the Wikipedia article finally jelled on the screen. Larry didn't bother to try "Hindu" in Wikipedia, just reached for Britannica volume H.

9

Sunday, five o'clock sharp. Larry stood on the porch of Anusheela's duplex, six-pack swinging from one hand, and rang the bell. It seemed to Larry that, with all the empty houses in town, no one should live in a duplex. But maybe Nan liked it that way. Her neighbour was another single mother and they could trade baby-sitting and so on. And, probably, it was good to have company. Larry wondered if she had managed to get a break on her rent. All these empty houses but rents remained at the same level they had reached before the mill shut down. Larry had read an explanation somewhere of why market forces hadn't influenced rents here and why that didn't mean there was something wrong with the market, but he found the argument incomprehensible and quit the article half-way through.

Balbir opened the door and glared up into Larry's face. A long moment passed, then Larry said, "Hey, Balbir, I think I'm expected."

Balbir shrugged. "Whatever." He stepped aside and yelled back. "Mom! That cop's here."

Anusheela looked in from the kitchen. "Sit down. I'll just be a moment." Larry handed her the beer. "Oh, thanks. You want one?"

Larry figured he should try to look as sober as possible. "Uh, I'll wait till supper."

"Okay."

Larry sat in an armchair. Balbir sprawled on the sofa. After thirty seconds of uncomfortable silence, he said, "That's my dad's chair."

"Right. You think he'd mind if I sat in it?"

"He hated cops."

"Really? He never told me that."

"You knew my dad?" Balbir was suspicious.

"Sure. Used to see him at the Century now and then." The New Century Hotel was the oldest building in Arcadia, built in 1900 when the town hoped to ride the silver boom that financed new cities all through south-eastern British Columbia. Most of the ones that hadn't switched to logging were now ghost towns. There were never many guests staying at the Century, except during LakeFest, but the lounge and beer parlor still functioned and the restaurant was competition for the Victory.

"Humph." Maybe Balbir meant to say something. Larry wondered how well he remembered his father. Balbir had only been four or five when Jogwinder left. Anusheela called them to supper. Glad that ordeal's over, Larry thought.

"So, how do you like biryani?"

"It's great!" And it was great. Larry was packing it in, rice and chicken and lots of spices. "I never had it before but it's really good! What are all the spices?"

"That's masala. And ginger and garlic and hot peppers. There is a story from long ago that a cook and a spice merchant had an accident together. They were going down the street in their carts and so on when they collided! All their things became mixed up. The cook had to make a dish for the king so he just cooked everything mixed, all the spices, everything, all together. The king loved it! And that was biryani."

"It's really good, Nan."

"Sometimes it has lamb, but that is hard to get here now."

"The chicken is really good."

"Really good," mimicked Balbir. His mother glared at him. For a second, Larry thought she might slap him. But the moment of parental discipline was interrupted by the telephone. Mouth set in a hard line, Anusheela moved to answer it.

Larry looked at Balbir. "It is really good. Don't you think so?"

"I bet you eat steaks," said Balbir, "And pork chops."

"Sometimes. Not that often. My parents were vegetarians."

Balbir's mouth hung open. Anusheela came back to the table. "It's for you, Larry."

"Oh, okay. Sorry." Who knew he was here? Scratch that. Probably everyone in town knew exactly where he was. "Hello?"

"Larry?" It was Fran. "There's an emergency. You need to get over to the Blaneys' house right now."

"Is it domestic again? Because Byron can handle that." Danny Byron was one of the auxiliary police officers that filled out the force. He was supposed to be taking calls.

"No. There's a death. Jim is already there. He wants you."

"A death… Mildred?"

"No. Doug. Sounds like someone beat him to death. You better go on over."

Larry put down the phone and glanced up across the room to see Balbir and Anusheela staring at him. "Death? Mildred?"

"No," said Larry, "Doug."

"Oh." Anusheela's face closed in comprehension. "I see." She knew immediately who had killed Doug Blaney. Well, no time to talk about that now.

"I'm sorry, Nan. I have to go. It was…"

"No, no. We understand. You go ahead. That's your job."

As he turned to go out the door, Larry caught the expression on Balbir's face. It wasn't respect exactly, but at least it wasn't a sneer.

10

"So what do you make of this, Doctor Watson?" Jim Tull squatted by the facedown body stretched out on the floor.

"Looks like someone bashed in the back of his head," said Larry.

"Elementary. And see this?" Tull pointed to the bloody shirttail that was pulled out of Blaney's pants.

"They wiped their hands?"

"So it seems. Pretty cold, eh?"

"Where is the weapon? Oh, never mind." Larry glimpsed a bloody stick underneath a chair. "Oh, Lord! Is that what I think it is?"

"Looks like a Fest-A-Rod to me," said Tull. "We'll pull it out after we take lots and lots of photographs. Plaskowitz went to get some cameras. Of course, to be certain, we'll have to match the blood and brains on the rod to whatever's left in Doug Blaney's head…" Tull shook his head. "Looks like he was hit over and over again. Probably knocked him down and kept going while he was on the floor." Tull pointed to dents in the carpet beside Blaney's head. "Somebody really hated the man."

"So, have you talked to her yet?"

Jim Tull rocked back on his heels. "Now who would that be, Watson?"

"You know who. Everybody in town knows who. And don't call me Watson."

"Well now, I deduce that you are suggesting that Mildred Blaney is the perpetrator of this horrific crime. Is that so, uh, Officer Kalmakoff?"

"For Christ's sake! Yes!"

"Then you might be interested in knowing that diligent police work has already established an alibi for the grieving widow. Of course, it needs to be fully checked out." Tull looked down at the corpse. "Because I grant you, if anyone benefits from this asshole's death, it's her."

"What kind of alibi?"

"Mildred Blaney was in a meeting over at the Fountain of Blood." Tull held up a hand. "Now before you ask, did she do this deed before attending that little prayer session, the answer is No." Tull paused, grinning.

"Okay, I'll bite. How do we know this?" Larry looked at the corpse and thought about body temperature and time of death.

"We know because the victim made a personal appearance at the church during the course of the meeting. Had a fight with his wife, too."

"Okay."

"Then he left, driven out by the harpy curses of the assembled women." Tull grinned, waiting.

"And Mildred stayed there."

"Right."

"The whole time."

"Correct. She was there when the body was discovered a couple of hours ago."

"And she never left?"

"Well, not according to the two women who were with her when we spoke. Of course, I don't have official statements yet from them." Tull was still grinning.

"There's more."

"There is. There is, in fact, a videotape or rather, nine videotapes, twenty minutes each, of the meeting. So, first thing when we're done here and we collect the statements of all concerned, we watch three hours of the meeting footage to see if Mildred Blaney ever ducks out long enough to do this."

"You have the tapes?"

"I do. And equipment to view them, on loan from our very own Steven Spielberg, Marcy Stoneman." Marcy was the wife of Councillor Jerry Stoneman. She also chaired the Arcadia cable TV co-operative that had built an antenna that picked up three broadcast channels. And, the co-op taped civic events that were shown, repeatedly, on the local access channel.

Tull glanced around. "Just waiting for Doctor Mendlesson now. Soon as he pronounces and we get the pictures taken, we'll check out the witnesses…"

"About the doctor…"

"Yes?" Tull saw that Larry was on to something and was suddenly alert, joking mannerisms gone.

"When they do the autopsy…"

"That won't be here. Mendlesson will have it shipped to Kelowna probably, maybe Cranbrook."

"Well, I'd like to know if there's any injury to the torso, like if someone jabbed the rod into Doug's stomach."

"Right." Tull nodded, "Did they Open the Door before they Lowered the Boom or whatever Starlight called it."

"Snap the Branch. Or Kill the Snake. Check his wrists, too. Though a broken bone there might be defensive. It might help to know if someone trained by Starlight did this."

"Good thinking. Okay, I'll make certain the doc knows to ask that question." Tull looked back down at the body then over at the Fest-A-Rod. "One thing, that's a well-made weapon. All this damage and it didn't even crack." He grinned up at Larry. "You got to be proud of our local craftsmen. I bet they sell millions of these things!"

"You think Mayor Wolichuk wants this advertised?"

"Now that's another question. Does the town want it known that a resident was beaten to death by gear meant to keep the peace during a local festival right before that festival happens? You think it would scare off the tourists? Get LakeFest cancelled?" Tull looked back down at the body. "Hell, maybe we should make certain the story gets out!"

11

"The last I saw, Doug was fine." Tear tracks marked Mildred Blaney's cheeks. Her voice was so quiet Larry had to strain to hear it. "Then Danny Byron called me."

"About a disturbance at your house?" Larry knew that Byron had taken the original call, a complaint about yelling and noise from the Blaney house. Nothing unusual.

"Well, he was already there. He found Doug and called to tell me."

Larry thought maybe he should have a word with Byron about notification and proper police procedure. Then he thought, the hell with it. What Byron did was probably the right thing to do in Arcadia.

The door of the little interview room burst open and two women strode in yelling. "You have no right to interrogate her like this! Think of what this woman has been through!"

And: "Where's her lawyer? Nothing she's told you is admissible! Nothing!" Rebecca Grant turned toward Mildred. "Not another word! I've called David Cantor!"

Janet Rimbert rounded on Larry. "How dare you! We were with Mildred the whole time! We know she didn't do anything and we'll both testify!"

Larry had a moment to reflect on the unlikely alliance of Rebecca Grant, Arcadia's most outspoken feminist, and Janet Rimbert, evangelical champion of Real Women and patriarchal values, before David Cantor charged through the door. "This woman is my client! Not another word, Mildred."

"I've already told her," snapped Rebecca Grant. She was a large woman who towered over Cantor.

"I'll take over now," he said. Larry admired the way the lawyer never backed away but stared right back up into Rebecca Grant's face.

"Okay," said Larry. "Everybody just hold on a minute."

All three, Rebecca, Janet, David, all turned on Larry, ready to attack, but Mildred's small voice interrupted. "He's just asking me a few questions. It's all right. He knows I didn't do anything."

Well, maybe, thought Larry, depending on how well your alibi holds up. "I need Mildred's statement," he said aloud, "And I need to ask about Doug, so we can find out who did this thing." He held up a hand to silence David Cantor. "Mildred, is this your lawyer?"

"I don't know. Do I need a lawyer?"

"You can have one if you want while I ask a few questions, but it's up to you to say who it will be."

"Oh, David's all right, I guess. I don't care. I just want to go home." Mildred's face fell as she thought about home and what was there.

Larry started, "Perhaps someplace else tonight…" Janet and Rebecca both spoke at once, offering a place to stay. "That's fine. Mildred will talk to you later. Right now you need to leave the room while I finish this up so Mildred can go rest, okay? Cantor, you can stay unless Mildred wants you to leave but try not to interrupt and drag things out, all right?" There was silence. There, thought Larry, sorted these people out. Then Janet, Rebecca, and David erupted again, shouting and gesturing at Larry and each other. Larry lost his temper and yelled back. Everyone was waving their arms and yelling when Mildred began swaying from side to side, then her eyes rolled back in her head and she collapsed face down on the table. The four conscious people in the room paused, then they all yelled at the same time: "See what *you* did!"

12

"Well? You want to run through them again?"

Larry looked at the stack of videocassettes, then shook his head. "Not now, Jim, my eyes are melting."

"Yeah. We need some sleep," said Tull. "But we agree on what we've seen, right?"

"Or didn't see." The two men had fast-forwarded through all nine tapes, pausing to rewind and play the section that recorded Doug Blaney's loud entrance to the meeting at the Fountain of Blood church. Mildred tried to quiet her husband but Blaney was too drunk to listen to her. Then other women in the group started yelling at him and, when Rebecca Grant rose from her chair and strode toward the man, Blaney beat a retreat. Comforted by other women, Mildred returned to her chair. "Blaney must have really upset Rebecca with all that yelling about whores and lesbians and all."

"Maybe," said Tull, "Is she lesbian?"

"I don't know. Hard core feminist, lives alone. Could be."

"Ask Fran, she knows everybody's sex life. What's Rebecca Grant doing at Janet Rimbert's church anyway?"

"Some LakeFest organizing thing. I don't know what they're planning exactly. I'll find out."

"Ask Rimbert?"

"After I get some sleep, maybe. Lord, what a bitch!"

"Man! You must be tired," said Tull, "Never heard you call anyone names like that."

"I meant this whole situation but after that session last night I feel like calling a lot of people names." Larry rubbed his face. "But you're right. I am tired. And I can't do any more of this now."

"Right. Anyway, it looks like Mildred Blaney's alibi checks out." They had fast-forwarded through the tapes, watching Mildred Blaney's pale face. The camera was set up at an angle to the rows of chairs so that whoever was speaking at the front of the group was on the left of the screen. Most of the chairs in the first few rows were visible. Mildred Blaney sat in the third row. After her husband stormed out, Mildred never left her seat. Many of the women came to sit with her and talk for a few minutes. Meanwhile, the clock on the wall, top center of the screen, showed a regular advance. An hour and thirty-eight minutes after Blaney left the hall, the telephone rang. Rebecca Grant picked it up and called Mildred over. Her face sagged with shock as she listened to Danny Byron's message, then Janet Rimbert guided her out of the room. Janet had driven Mildred to her house. "How long a drive is it?"

Tull shrugged. "Five minutes? What is it, six blocks? Eight? You could walk it in ten."

"Maybe a five minute round trip. Another minute to beat Blaney's head in. So six minutes is all the time she'd need."

"Larry, Mildred Blaney goes and sits in that chair after Doug leaves and doesn't move for even six seconds. And there isn't more than a minute lost between tapes when they changed them. At least if the clock doesn't lie. And I sure didn't see the hands suddenly jump forward or back or anything, did you?"

"No. But I guess that's what we have to look at next. Make sure that second hand sweeps once a minute like it's supposed to."

"I kept checking. Regular as clockwork, seems to me." Tull waited. "You didn't even react to that at all."

"I'm going home and go to bed. After I wake up, I'll tell you what I think of your lousy jokes."

"Okay. Just making sure you weren't already unconscious. I'm going home, too. Fran can look after the town. Fran and Plaskowitz."

"Oh, Lord. Look, I'll be back in a few hours. Just a nap, that's all I need."

Tull grinned. "All I have to do is mention Plaskowitz and you get all jumpy. Don't worry, he's not a complete moron." Larry got up to go. "Seriously, Larry, get some sleep. This isn't going anywhere and you need to get as much rest as possible before LakeFest gets going."

"Oh, Lord! I had managed to forget about that for a little while."

Tull laughed. "Sweet dreams."

13

Larry fell into bed. Suddenly, he awoke. For a moment he thought that he hadn't slept at all, just closed his eyes and opened them again. It was dark and Larry sat up and grabbed the clock at his bedside. Two AM. He had been asleep a good ten hours! Larry groaned, climbed out of bed, and called the station. "Danny? This is Larry. Anything going on?"

"No," said Byron, "Everything is quiet. What's the trouble?"

"Nothing. I should be there, that's all."

"Chief revised the roster. Doesn't have you in until eight."

"Oh. Sorry."

"Hey, no problem. I can use the hours."

"Well, I'll be down pretty soon anyway. Soon as I get dressed."

"No rush."

Larry pulled his uniform from the chair where he had thrown it the night before. He took his gun from the lockbox and went out to the car. No time for coffee, he'd get a cup of the station brew. He locked his gun in the compartment beside the driver's seat and backed out of his driveway. Larry headed toward the station but hadn't gone half a block before changing his mind. He picked up the mike and radioed Byron, "Danny, I'm in the car. Gonna do a cruise."

"10-4." Byron responded. He loved the cop talk he'd picked up from TV.

Larry turned at the next corner and headed uphill, through Dogpatch, looking for signs that people were camping in the abandoned houses. Then he drove downtown and cruised the alley behind Main Street, shining his spot on all the store back entrances, checking for broken locks or doors ajar. He circled the schoolyard looking for dopers, and the used car lot, seeing if vagrants were sleeping there. Finally, when he was certain that everything was okay in his town, Larry drove on to the police station.

"Still nothin' happening, Larry."

"Okay. I'm going to take another look at those videotapes."

"Sure."

Larry drew a cup of coffee from the urn and sat down in front of the monitor. Marcy Stoneman had loaned them her own VCR, similar to the one used to record the meeting. Larry slipped in a tape and set the timer to 00:00. The tape began playing and he noted the time on the clock: 2:13. He fast-forwarded ten minutes and checked the clock again: 2:23. Doug Blaney made his entrance, ranting, yelling at Mildred, yelling at all the women. Then he was gone. At 21:09 the tape ended. The clock on the wall read 2:34. Larry put in the next tape. Now the clock said 2:35. He fast-forwarded five minutes: 2:40. Five more minutes: 2:45. And so it went. The clock never faltered, Mildred never left her chair. Then came the phone call. You could hear the ring on the tape. A young woman, one of Dolphin Starlight's protégés, was speaking to the group. Rebecca Grant picked up the receiver. She signalled to Mildred who walked over, listened for a moment, and asked a horrified question. All the other noise in the room ceased. All heads turned toward Mildred Blaney. "Thank you," she said in her small, quiet voice. "I'll be there soon as I can."

Rebecca pounced. "Do you need a ride, Mildred?"

"Yes, please, Becky. Something's happened to Doug." She looked up with an agonized expression. "They say he's dead!" The clock said 4:12.

"I'll get my car," said Rebecca but it was Janet Rimbert who led Mildred from the room.

Danny Byron was looking over Larry's shoulder. "I got the call about three forty, a little after. Liz Honeycutt, she lives next door. She's usually the one that calls about the Blaneys. Or did. I didn't hurry. Got there at 3:50. Found the body. Called Tull first, then the doc. Called a couple other people before I found out where Mildred was."

The tape ran out. Marcy had put in a new one, the ninth, and continued to record the meeting. It was ten after five before people stopped milling about and began leaving. Larry made a list of the eighteen faces he recognized and noted the three that he didn't, including the hippy girl who was speaking when the telephone rang.

"That's it," said Larry.

"You got it figured out?" Byron stared at him in wonder.

"No. I'm saying, that's it, Mildred Blaney has an alibi."

Byron looked at the dark monitor. "No way!"

"Way. Now, I'm going to go get some breakfast."

14

"The usual?"

"Sure. Uh, wait, Nan. Hold the sausage. Just the eggs and toast, okay?"

Anusheela paused, looked around to make sure no one was listening, then leaned toward Larry. "I eat bacon, you know." Larry's jaw dropped. "Well, not all the time, you understand, but once in a while. I find it very tasty, too. It's not really meat, I think, something all by itself."

"A new food group."

"Yes. Like chocolate!"

"Right. Well, uh, the usual with bacon, then."

"Okay. It was good to have you over."

"I'm sorry I had to run out last night…"

"In actual fact, it was the night before."

"Oh. Yes. I'm a little turned around. But I enjoyed it, Nan, and I'd like to try again for an uninterrupted dinner. Or maybe I could take you and Balbir out or something."

"That would be very nice."

"Or maybe a barbecue."

"Balbir would love that."

"It won't be until after LakeFest is finished, I'm afraid."

"I understand. It's coming on quickly now." Anusheela glanced up, saw Bob Weber walking in. "I will get your breakfast." She paused. "Will you be arresting her soon?"

"Mildred? Nan, I don't think we'll be arresting her at all."

Anusheela smiled. "Oh, good. You get an extra piece of bacon for that!"

Bob Weber slid onto the bench across the table as Anusheela left. "Well, this is a terrible day for Arcadia. Terrible!" Weber shook his head. "A fine citizen like that arrested."

"Like who, Bob?" Larry knew that Weber was fishing for information and had already decided to give him some. Start a good rumor for a change, he thought. But for now, let Bob do his fishing.

"Well, like poor Mildred Blaney. All those years… Sooner or later, something snaps!"

"Something snaps?"

"You know what I'm talking about! Never speak ill of the dead, but… Poor Doug! And just the other morning we all had breakfast together." Weber shook his head. "Just goes to show…"

"Yes. Wasn't that when Doug was describing how to gun down the audience at LakeFest?"

"Not exactly, Larry, no. He was talking about security measures, that's all."

"So why do you think he was killed?"

"Well, poor Mildred… I mean, everybody knows… That is…" Weber suddenly realized that he was answering a policeman's questions. Anusheela brought a pot of coffee over to the table and Weber seized the opportunity to shut up. Larry let him stew in silence for a few seconds. That was all Bob Weber could take, "So, do you think the judge will be lenient?"

"What judge, Bob?"

"The one trying Mildred Blaney, of course!"

Anusheela set down a plate of eggs and sausage and bacon in front of Larry. "Trying Mildred? I thought you said…"

"First I heard of a trial, Nan, but it sounds like Bob here has some inside information."

"Oh, I see." Anusheela decided to help things along. "From the business community, no doubt."

Weber tried to grasp the situation. "Now, wait, haven't you…aren't you going to arrest Mildred Blaney?"

"Why on earth would I do that, Bob?"

"Well, didn't she… Doug is dead, right?"

"Yes, Bob, he is. And if you have any information to share with the police, I'd love to hear it." Larry wore his most serious, solemn expression.

"Well, I… No, I don't know anything. No!" Weber shut up, this time for a full five minutes. Anusheela's eyes were twinkling like stars when Larry paid his cheque. He couldn't remember when he had enjoyed his breakfast more.

15

"So, how did it go?"

"There's nothing there, Fran. Her alibi stands up."

"Not Mildred Blaney, I know she didn't murder her jerk of a husband, I meant your dinner at Anusheela's."

"Well, it was going great, until I got your phone call and left for the Blaney house."

"Uh-huh. Impressed the boy, I bet."

"Maybe. Fran, how do you know Mildred didn't kill Doug?"

"Mildred Blaney kill someone? That woman wouldn't swat a fly without permission!" Fran shook her head. "There's no way she would raise her voice to Doug, much less beat his head in."

"Okay, so who did kill him?"

"Well, now you're asking me to start a rumour and I won't do that. I'll just say that no one in town is shedding any tears over this." Fran reflected a moment. "Except Mildred, of course. The woman has no sense. Mind you, if she did have any sand in her bucket she would have dumped that jerk long ago."

Jim Tull entered the station. Fran's mouth pursed up like she smelled something bad. Fran didn't seem to like Tull at all. That put her in company with a lot of others. Council saw the police chief as a walking expense item, of course, but Larry couldn't figure out what Fran's complaint was. Tull fought for her salary demands and always backed his staff and their decisions.

"Thought you might still be in bed, Sunshine," Tull greeted Larry.

"Didn't mean to sleep so long…"

Tull was checking the log. "Jesus, you came on at 2 AM!" Tull and Fran both stared at Larry as though he was some strange life form hitherto unknown to science.

"Yeah. I wanted to go over those tapes. And I did a patrol, too."

Tull shook his head. "That's really something, Larry. Well, anything turn up either place?"

"No. I'm pretty certain Mildred was at that meeting when Doug was killed."

"Yeah," said Tull, "Me, too. Now what?"

"I don't know. I still need to interview Mildred about Doug's enemies…"

"Shouldn't take more than a couple of days to recite all their names."

"Maybe. Nobody liked the guy, but who hated him? I mean, hate him enough to kill him like that? There was that guy he beat up in the bar a year or so ago, but he left town and hasn't been back. Might be others like that."

"Okay," Tull nodded. "I expect Cantor will allow you to talk to his client on that basis."

"I'll phone him, ask him for an interview at Mildred's convenience, tell him why."

"Good. Then there's Marcy Stoneman who taped this thing, and the two who tried to help her after she got Danny's call. They seem to know Mildred. And I think we need to talk with the people living around the Blaneys. Maybe somebody saw something. Hell," said Tull, "Maybe we'll get lucky and find Doug surprised a burglar, some stranger from out of town we won't feel bad about sending to prison just because he killed Doug Blaney."

"Maybe."

"Right. It would have to be somebody really disgusting, wouldn't it?"

Larry, Fran, and Tull silently contemplated the notion, trying to think of someone people might want to convict for killing Doug Blaney. "Ted Bundy?"

Tull shook his head. "I understand that guy could be real charming sometimes."

"A psycho with no charm? Robert Pickton?"

"Maybe. Some people would say Blaney's killer did the world a favour."

"But," said Larry, "What did Doug do to make people hate him so?" Fran and Tull silently turned their heads to stare into Larry's face. "Well, outside of being an asshole and an obnoxious gun freak and a nasty drunk and bullying Mildred, I mean. Is that enough cause to beat a man to death?" Fran and Jim Tull continued to stare at Larry. They didn't say a word.

16

"So, Ms. Stoneman..."

"For God's sake, Larry, call me Marcy!"

Marcy Stoneman had been Prom Queen but Jack wasn't allowed to be King, because he had dropped out to play hockey. When Marcy abandoned the Prom to run off with Jack, it was just about the most romantic moment that Arcadia had ever experienced. But that was years in the past and Marcy's wide teenage eyes had narrowed into housewife slits. They had no children. It was rumored that Jack was at fault.

"Right. Okay. So, Marcy, I want to ask about the meeting at the Fountain of Blood Church."

"You saw the tapes, didn't you?"

"Yes. Yes, I did," said Larry.

"So why in hell are you asking me stuff?"

"Marcy, we're trying to understand the tapes. Like, when Doug came into the meeting, what was he angry about?"

"Women!"

"Women?"

"Well, you must have heard some of it. He said women were stupid and nosy and gossipy and too dumb to understand the problems they were causing." Marcy took a breath. "Only he never said 'women', he said 'bitches'' a lot, and other words. I think he said 'females' once or twice."

"So why was he mad at women?"

"For God's sake! This is Doug Blaney! He's mad about everything. I always thought he might murder somebody, never thought he'd be the one to die." Marcy paused and shook her head and Larry jumped in.

"Was he mostly yelling at Mildred?"

"Oh, I think he had some rage for everyone there. Spread the wealth, you know."

"Did he mention specific women?"

"Well, that I couldn't tell you." Marcy clammed up. There were whole seconds of silence. Larry wondered if Marcy knew more than she was saying.

"And you were behind the camera the whole time."

"Yes. Changing tapes in the machine, watching the audio. Of course I came out to talk to Mildred." She stopped. "That's on tape, I bet."

"Yes, it is."

"Wait a minute! Do you think I left the camera running and ran out and killed Doug Blaney and then ran back to change tapes?"

"Well, I was wondering..."

"Because that's just too damn stupid for anyone to believe, even the Arcadia police."

"Actually, I was wondering how much you saw that maybe the camera didn't pick up. Like if anyone else left and came back."

"My God! You are that stupid! Well, Officer, I didn't see anybody leave and come back with blood all over them. Does that answer your question?"

17

Larry stepped outside the interview room and took a deep breath. Jim Tull emerged from his office. "You get anything?"

"Just an assessment of my intelligence, that's all. Haven't asked her about offering Mildred a ride yet."

"Right," said Tull, "Well, I got nothing either except heartfelt prayers that I will burn in hell." There was only one interview room, so Tull had been talking to Janet Rimbert in his office.

"She wants you to burn? She's not trying to save you?"

Tull spread his hands. "Near as I can figure, Janet has already consigned me to the fifteenth circle of hell. The one reserved for cops named Jim."

"Right."

"You want to switch? You know what they say, change is as good as a rest."

"I could use a rest."

"Me too. Well," Tull gestured at his office door, "Abandon hope and enter there."

Janet Rimbert was small and quick and very angry at being in the Arcadia police station. She glared at Larry, her body swaying from side to side, and whenever he asked a question, Janet snapped her head forward, like she was going to take a bite out of his words.

"Janet, I'm just trying to find out what happened, that's all."

"Then why ask me? I was at the meeting."

"Yes, but that's what I'm trying to ask about."

"I never saw anyone leave. No one!"

"And..."

"And I don't know why Doug was so angry except that he was always angry. Always!"

"All right. Well..."

Janet Rimbert brought her hands together and closed eyes. "Lord, help this all to be right. Help all those who need protection. Bring blindness and confusion to those who would countenance suffering." She went on a minute or two, then sat face down, hands in her lap Larry figured she was finished praying.

"Janet, you offered Mildred a ride? When she got the phone call? About his death?"

"I drove her home. The police were already there. You know that."

"Yes. Janet, did Mildred say anything to you in the car..."

Janet dropped her face in her hands and began praying. This was the third time she had prayed since Larry had entered the room. He studied Janet's thin arms and wondered if she had the strength to kill someone with a club. Veins and sinew writhed in her forearms as she worked her hands, twisting prayerful words from the air. Yes, Larry thought, she had all the strength she needed in those knotty arms. The questioning was useless. I am blind and confused, thought Larry. I don't countenance suffering, I think, but does Janet Rimbert believe that I do? Time to end this.

18

"Well," said Tull, "Still blessed? Or headed to the fiery depths?"

"I don't know," said Larry, "I don't mind being prayed *for*, but being prayed *at*, is a bit much."

"I feel your pain, Larry. I got nothing from Marcy Stoneman either."

"Jim, is it possible that we're just wasting time here? I mean, anyone could have walked into Blaney's house and killed him. Doesn't have to be one of the women at the meeting. None of them had blood on them that I could see."

"True. And we need to keep an open mind, but..." Tull shrugged. "We still have to interview them. Last people to see Doug alive and all."

"Yeah. And there's something..."

"Right. Now hold that thought, Watson, because Rebecca Grant is next on the docket." He grinned. "And you take the interview, Larry, because I think she's called you a sexist pig a few less times than she's called me that."

"Uh, when did she ever call me..?"

"There! You see? You're the man for this job."

"Oh, Lord!" I'm a sinner, thought Larry, Janet Rimbert would condemn my taking the Lord's name in vain, but, oh Lord.

Rebecca Grant sat with her arms folded across her chest. Her checked lumberjack shirt, also known as a Canadian tuxedo, was open and she wore a blue work shirt underneath. Pretty hot to be wearing so many clothes, but Rebecca always dressed that way, summer and winter.

"So you were at the meeting to, uh..."

"To set up a place where women can feed their babies without upsetting men with the sight of their bare breasts."

"Right. Yes."

"Because it's so disgusting or arousing or whatever."

"I, uh, see."

"We didn't have a name yet. We wanted something that had 'Safe' in it. Because if you call something a Safe Place, then men know to stay away." Rebecca stopped and considered. "Unless they're gay. Or PTSD. There was talk about a separate Safe Place for men, but then we couldn't decide whether to separate the gays from the PTSD, because they might not get along. Then we got back to the space for women. Let the men find their own place!"

"Okay..."

"That what you wanted to know? That's what the meeting was doing when Blaney arrived."

"Yes. I'd like..."

"That jerk yelled and stomped around and made a fuss, like men do when they can't get their way. And, afterwards, that was all we talked about, so I guess that tactic worked. Again."

"What was he yelling about?"

"He was just swearing at women. I don't think he believed that women should be allowed to get together in groups. I don't know."

"Was his anger directed at Mildred?"

"Nope. He insulted every woman who ever walked the face of the earth."

"No. I mean..."

"I know what you fucking meant. My answer stands."

"Okay." Larry fumbled for a question. "So, after Doug left, who stayed behind?"

"Stayed? We all stayed. Oh, you want to know if anyone sneaked out and killed Blaney." Rebecca leaned back and narrowed her eyes. "You think I would tell you if I thought someone there did it? You think I would rat out a sister?"

"Well..."

Rebecca sat back and considered. One thing about her, thought Larry, she always considers both sides. Sometimes it meant not making a decision, but Rebecca Grant was fair.

"It's possible," she said finally. "If I knew a woman was a murderer, I might turn her in, especially if the victim was another woman. But Doug Blaney?" She snorted a laugh.

Very fine appreciation of justice there, thought Larry. A thought struck him. "Did you train with the, uh, Fest-A-Rods?"

"Hell, no. I don't need a stick to defend myself!" Rebecca Grant was a large woman, more than six feet tall and out-weighing Larry by probably twenty pounds. She glowered at him.

Larry was struck by the fact that he didn't feel intimidated at all. Rebecca Grant looked imposing, but she wasn't frightening, you didn't have the feeling that she might suddenly grab you by the throat, like you did with Janet Rimbert or Marcy Stoneman, even though they were much smaller. On the other hand, you could picture her coming up from behind and beating someone's brains in.

Rebecca announced, "Janet Rimbert is just looking to make a buck."

"Uh, okay..."

"Well, all right, but..." Grant considered the situation. "There's nothing wrong with that! Women can make money, too, you know."

"Well, it's that you sound a little, uh, conflicted. Is the violence..?"

Rebecca leaned forward. "Men are violent! Women are victims!" She sat back. "Until they learn how to fight back."

"Okay. So you offered Mildred a ride home."

"Yes, but she went with Janet Rimbert. I followed." Rebecca waited. "Is that important?"

"Probably not."

"She didn't stay with me that night either. Or with Janet Rimbert. I don't know where she stayed."

Larry kept quiet. He knew that Mildred was staying with Fran Doucet. Of course, that wasn't a secret that could be kept very long in Arcadia, but a cousin in the Okanagan had offered Mildred a place to stay and she would be headed there pretty soon.

"Nothing," said Larry, "I got nothing."

"Okay, Watson."

"Jim, we have to interview them all! All the women that were there!"

"I know. But today was the hardest." Tull looked thoughtful. "I think. Might be a few other difficult interviews." He brightened. "Anyway, we're done with that right now. We're overdue at a meeting with Council."

"Council?"

"I believe they're considering firing us." Tull grinned. "At least we can hope that's what they're considering."

"Yeah," said Larry, "I'm ready to be fired."

"There you go. Look on the bright side."

"I am. I'm thinking it would be great not to have to police LakeFest."

Tull didn't say anything. He just nodded.

19

"So the question we've got up in the air here is whether or not to ask the RCMP for help." Mayor Wolichuk looked from one to another of the city councillors, then to Jim Tull. "Chief?"

"Two things: first, I believe the Arcadia police can handle this matter." Pete Rimbert snorted. Tull continued, "It appears to be a local person that committed this crime and the local force should be better at figuring out who…"

"We know who it was!"

David Cantor stood up and went at Pete Rimbert, "I need to know right now, are you referring to my client? Because if there's a conflict here…" Rimbert was a tall, muscular man, rangy and hard-looking, especially when set against the small lawyer, but Cantor leaned right into him.

Tull began speaking again. He spoke in a quiet, firm manner, not making jokes, wanting people to recognize the seriousness of this matter. "Your client is not a suspect, Mr. Cantor. In fact, at this time, we have no suspects."

"Right," said Rimbert, "Still fumbling around for clues."

"We are questioning the Blaneys' neighbours to find out if they saw anyone unusual in the area. And we are waiting on the medical examiner's report. Maybe that will suggest an investigative approach. But, the second thing I wanted to say, if you do decide to call in the Mounties, we will cooperate with them one hundred percent."

"Yeah," sneered Rimbert, "Maybe we should call them in one hundred percent of the time."

"That's a local government decision," said Tull. "If you want the RCMP instead of a local police force, then you can ask the province for a contract."

Everyone around the table was silent. Contracting the RCMP as the local police force would cost Arcadia far more than the town was currently spending. For one thing, the Mounties would insist on adding staff to meet established standards and each one of those officers would receive a lot more pay than Arcadia was currently handing out, not to mention the increase in pension contributions and employee benefits. If the population dropped below the magical number of 5000, then the Province would pick up the bill for policing Arcadia. Of course, no one wanted any more population loss. Everyone was still hoping the community could recover, somehow, and grow back to its old size. Still, at least once a year, Council looked into the relative cost between keeping the police and hiring the RCMP.

"Now that is another question for a different discussion," said Wolichuk, "and we need to focus on the sense of this meeting before us."

There was a moment of silence as people deciphered the Mayor's words, then Jerry Stoneman said, "Of course, if the Mounties do come, they'd probably still be here during LakeFest and that might cause some difficulties." Everyone understood what he meant. The RCMP would insist on the same amount of work and cooperation from the local force as if it was fully manned and had enough personnel to handle a major festival. They might issue a negative report to the Attorney-General's office, saying that Arcadia's music festival needed more security, more police. Of course, a security firm wouldn't be using Fest-A-Rods, so Jerry Stoneman would be against the idea. "On the other hand," said Stoneman, "They might wrap this up right away. Maybe." He sat back and allowed the doubt to percolate in the minds of Council.

"All right," said Rimbert, "So the Mounties might get rid of the murder situation, but then we'd be stuck with them as police." He thought for a minute. "They wouldn't use Fest-A-Rods, either. The rods wouldn't have a chance." He threw up his hands." Okay. We're stuck with the Keystone Cops. All right." He folded his arms and looked disgusted.

"Now, Pete," said Mayor Wolichuk, "That's not at all what I've been hearing and I've been listening at every angle here. This terrible crime should not keep the citizens of Arcadia from normal pursuits of gainful pleasure. If we allow this regrettable death to stop LakeFest then the murderer will claim another victim."

"That is the truth, Your Worship," said Jerry Stoneman.

The mayor went on, "We can't let this murder grow! But, after LakeFest, we'll take another look at this business because there are two minds here and we want to bring them together in the same direction."

Council formed the mayor's words into a motion and voted. David Cantor abstained. Otherwise the votes were all in favour: No Mounties at least until after LakeFest was over and maybe not then. My job was saved by Fest-A-Rods, thought Larry. The combination of the rods and a stingy Council meant he was going to be working LakeFest. Oh well, maybe something else would come up and he'd be fired. There was always hope.

20

"It was just after four. I was at the workbench there when I heard the yelling." Liz Honeycutt shook her head. Her hair was white, but thick and braided into a long pigtail down her back. "It happens all the time. I guess you know that." Larry nodded. "Well I'm never sure. I keep thinking, this time he's really going to hurt her. I mean, she's been hurt, but this time really bad. You understand."

Larry understood. Mildred Blaney had suffered a cracked cheekbone, a broken rib, a fractured wrist, and lost a tooth. But that was her toll over many years of abuse. Generally, Doug stopped before he crossed a certain line. But you never knew, the next time might be the one when he beat Mildred to death.

"And it is her fault, too! Not that she deserves the beatings, but that she doesn't leave him! And why not? We all told her, offered her help. Oh, that's a terrible thing to say, that it's her fault. There's this Battered Wife Syndrome and all but... Oh, My!"

Larry didn't say anything but, silently, he agreed. All the resources of this small town had been offered Mildred, had been pressed on her at one time or other, but she always went back to Doug. Larry tried to be sensitive around these issues, he knew about Battered Wife Syndrome, too, but deep down, he couldn't stifle the notion that Mildred was partly to blame for her situation.

"Anyway, I usually listen a little while to the yelling and stuff breaking and try to judge if this is a time I should call. She never makes a sound, not ever. All the yelling comes from him. Came from him. Whatever. I know Mildred is going to say she fell down the stairs or something but, still, once the police get there, the hitting stops." Liz Honeycutt glared at Larry.

"Took them long enough to get here this time, I have to say."

"About ten minutes…"

Liz snorted. "I could do it faster even without a car." Liz Honeycutt was in a wheelchair. She had been one of the town's original hippies, arriving about 1970, and supported herself through sales of jewellery made from local materials. One day, while Liz was hunting rocks and driftwood on the beach near the mill, a log dropped loose from a grapple, bounced end over end, and struck Liz in the back. She hadn't walked since. The company wasn't liable since Liz was in a posted area, but gave her a forty-five thousand dollar settlement anyway to head off any lawsuits. Liz used the money to buy a house. At LakeFest, she had a booth where she sold her crafted jewellery.

"Anyway, I was at the table there," She gestured toward the work area where she polished rocks and strung together chunks of driftwood from the lake. "I stopped working like I always do when these fights happened…"

"How often was that?"

"Oh, maybe every three or four weeks or so, but they only got big enough to call the police two or three times a year. At least, in my judgment."

"Were they getting worse?"

Liz reflected. "No. I think there's been about the same intensity for the last twenty years or more. And about the same frequency. Didn't even change when the mill shut down. That had me worried, you know."

"You mean you thought Dave might take out his unemployment on Mildred."

"Yes. But it didn't happen. It was like they had a routine or something." Liz clapped a hand to her face. "Oh, My! I don't mean that Mildred arranged these fights. Or timed them."

"No. I understand." Larry wondered if he did. "Go on. What made you think it was time to call the police?"

'Well, timing was part of it. It's been a while since Mildred went to the hospital… Oh, that sounds so bad!"

"I understand."

"Okay. And then the yelling kept getting louder, like it was building up to something. Then it stopped completely. I thought he was just hitting her then."

"But now you think what?"

"Well, I guess that's when she was killing him. Anyway, that's when I phoned. I guess, even if the police had got here sooner, he would've been dead already."

"You think it was Mildred who killed him?"

"Who else?"

"Did you hear her say anything? Yell? Cry out?"

"No. Like I said, she's always been quiet." Liz looked up at Larry. "You mean she didn't do it?"

"Mildred is not a suspect at this time," Larry said carefully.

A little smile flickered at the edge of Liz Honeycutt's mouth. "Well, I'll be damned. Good on her!" She looked up and her smile broadened. "I guess there's not much else I can tell you, Officer." And right then Larry knew that he would not get another thing from Liz Honeycutt.

21

"So, nothing from the neighbours except their hearty congratulations to the widow on her recent bereavement," said Tull.

"Yes," said Larry, "That's about it."

"Okay. Well, Cantor's bringing her down for a chat in a few minutes."

"Great."

"You got anything you want to try to work here?"

"No. You?"

"Nope. Just see if she's got any ideas, that's all. Man!" said Tull, "We're really scraping the bottom of the barrel."

"Let's get some ground rules straight," said David Cantor. Mildred Blaney sat meekly beside him.

Tull held up a hand. "Look, counsellor, for the record, your client is not a suspect, okay?" He turned toward Mildred, "So far as we are concerned, you were at the church hall when Doug was killed. What we want to know is, can you tell us who might have done it?"

"No." Mildred's voice was so soft and quiet, both Larry and Tull leaned across the table to listen.

"Now, Mildred, do you know anyone who might have wanted to hurt Doug?"

"No."

"Was Doug involved in any business deals recently?"

Mildred's eyes widened. "I don't know." She looked to Cantor for help.

"Ms.Blaney has no knowledge of her husband's business affairs."

"Doug always said I shouldn't think about that stuff. He said that was Man work."

"All right. Well, who was your husband talking to in the last while? Who did he hang out with?"

"Oh, Doug never hung out or anything."

"Was there anyone he liked to talk to?"

"No. He didn't like to talk much."

This was going nowhere, thought Larry. "Mildred, when Doug came over to the church, what was he angry about? What was he yelling about?"

"I don't know. When he yells I can't understand him. I just see him there, his mouth moving, and I can't hear at all. It's like it all goes silent. And then… and then…" Mildred's voice dwindled away.

"I think that's enough." Cantor's voice was like a sudden shout in Larry's ear. Larry realized that he was halfway across the table trying to pick up a sound from Mildred's slowly moving lips.

"It's all my fault." Did Mildred say that or was he trying too hard to make sense of the whimpering noises coming from her mouth? Larry slid back across the table into his chair.

"Just a second…" Tull began.

"No. You can see how distressed my client is. That's all for now. If you have any more questions, please submit them in writing."

"What? No!"

"Okay," said Cantor, "That's it! We're going!"

"Just… Wait, Mr. Cantor, you see what we're after here." Larry tried to get Cantor to sit back down.

"Come on, Mildred, we're getting out of here." Mildred Blaney still sat staring straight ahead, her mouth still moving.

"Okay," said Larry, "But see if you can get her to come up with a name. Please. Come on, Cantor, we're on the same side here."

The lawyer looked Larry in the eye. "No," he said, "We're not."

"But surely Mildred wants to know who killed her husband. I mean, maybe the killer will come after her."

David Cantor cocked his head and curled his lip, "Oh, right. Someone after the Blaney fortune, no doubt," he said sarcastically.

Larry couldn't think of anything more to say as Cantor escorted his client from the police station.

"She looks pretty bad," said Tull.

"Yeah. Mildred's always been meek but now she looks really broken."

"You think she's on meds?"

"Maybe," said Larry. "I think I need to read up on this battered wife thing. How do they feel once their battering husband is dead? Maybe it totally messes their heads around."

"You think psychoanalyzing Mildred is going to help us figure out who killed Doug?"

"Well, what else do we have to work with?"

Fran Doucet stuck her head in the door. "Autopsy report is here."

22

"Lord! Look at that blood alcohol. Point one nine! I'm surprised the guy could even walk!"

"Hmm," said Tull, "Look here. Total blows to skull estimated to be fourteen, give or take a couple. Um, '…extensive fracturing…brain exposed…' Um, here. See this? One blow striking the left rear parietal. Came up behind Blaney and swung across, see" Tull brought his arm around. "Bop! A right-handed killer? Or a lefty with a two-handed swing? Hell! Anyway, then one right square on the top of his head, maybe while he was on his knees. Then the rest."

```
The medical evidence would suggest
that the victim went to his knees
immediately after the first blow and
then face forward on the floor
following the second. All other blows
occurred while the victim was prone.
The remaining blows to the head,
```

perhaps twelve or more, are
concentrated in the specified area.
They are very forceful blows and
appear to have all been aimed at the
victim's head. There are no injuries
to any other part of the body.

"These all from above, aimed at the upper rear cranium. Someone standing over him, see, banging away, probably two-handers." Tull demonstrated. "He gets whacked, falls to his knees. Whack again! Blaney tips forward on his face and the guy stood over him just whaling away with the Fest-A-Rod. Man!" Tull shook his head. "Lot of anger there."

"From behind?"

"Yep. And no marks on any part of the body except his skull. So there goes the Dolphin Starlight connection."

"I want to ask him about this anyway. Even if this is outside regular training, maybe he's showing people how to Hit the Snake from behind."

"And Crack de Coconut, eh? Maybe. Go on and talk to him."

"<u>Back</u> of the head! No! Absolutely not!" Dolphin Starlight had a look of utter disgust on his face. "The idea is for people to be able to face a troublesome person, even someone that's armed, *face* them with confidence. Not to sneak up behind them and beat them to death!" Dolphin shook his head. "A person who would do that… Well, the spiritual ramifications are enormous. Enormous!" He stared off into the distance, eyes wide with horror.

"Okay," said Larry, "I understand. So, did anyone at your training sessions seem, oh, a little too eager."

"What do you mean?"

"Well, did anyone seem to be the kind of person who might enjoy beating someone else with a stick?"

"There's no one here like that!"

Larry persisted. "Did you send anyone away or…"

"No! The only person to drop out of training was Mildred Blaney." Dolphin sighed. "Actually, if I asked anyone to leave, it would have been her."

"Oh?"

"Even after hours of training and drill, she had no confidence whatsoever. I suggested that she look at another area to volunteer her services. Aloe took her to a child-care organizing session."

"Aloe?"

"Like the healing plant. There she is over there." Dolphin gestured toward a young barefoot woman wearing a loose one-piece dress. Larry recognized her from the videotape as the person speaking to the women when the phone call about Blaney's death came through.

"I think I might have a word with her."

Dolphin shrugged. "Go ahead."

"What was she organizing again?"

"Ask her yourself."

Okay, Mr. Starlight. Larry walked over to the young woman. "Aloe?" She turned and smiled up into Larry's face. It was an open smile, wide and warm below deep, understanding eyes and, for a moment, Larry knew that peace which passeth understanding. "Um, Hi! My name's Larry Kalmakoff. I wonder if we could talk a bit."

Aloe shifted her body and allowed an expression of inquiry to slide into her smile. For the first time, Larry noticed the naked infant that Aloe clasped in one arm. "What do you want to talk about?"

"You were at the Fountain of Blood meeting three days ago?"

"Yes."

"What was the meeting about?"

"We were organizing infant care." She smiled and Larry felt himself falling into her understanding eyes. One touch from Aloe, he thought, one understanding touch would heal every hurt that he had suffered in his entire life. Aloe's soft lips parted and words flowed from them. "There is day care and events for older children, but we need a place where mothers can change diapers and so on. A place where women can sit in the shade a little while. You know, you can get pretty tired carrying a baby everywhere."

"I understand," said Larry. And, for a moment, he did understand, he understood the eternal suffering of women and the wonder of their patient nurturing.

"And feed their babies. Some people get upset at breastfeeding in public, you know. We don't want people to be uncomfortable." Aloe kept smiling and allowed her dress to slide off one shoulder and reveal a luscious round breast. She took her time about getting the nipple into her baby's mouth and Larry realized he was being gamed. Suddenly Aloe looked a lot less attractive.

"Okay, you have a tent set up where women can bring their babies. So what was Mildred Blaney's job?"

"She hadn't been assigned one yet. She only came to that one meeting."

"You suggested this baby-care work to her after security training didn't work out?"

"I guess. Dolphin mentioned something about Mildred's problem to me, her lack of confidence and so on, and I talked to her. I don't know if she'd completely given up on the other thing, though. She took her rod home with her."

Where somebody used it to kill Doug Blaney. "What was Blaney yelling at Mildred about?"

"I don't know. I thought he was yelling at all of us. He called us sluts and the C-word, he used that a lot."

"Why?"

"I don't know." Aloe turned up her understanding face to Larry and said, "I believe he was just using all the bad names for women that he could think of."

"So he was upset that this was a meeting of women?"

Aloe shrugged, "Maybe. Maybe he wanted Mildred to go back to the security job."

Was that it? Blaney wanted his wife to be more assertive and learn how to use a weapon? It didn't make sense.

23

"Say, Watson, want to hear something peculiar?"

It was morning at the LakeFest grounds. People were beginning to set up, but everything was still quiet and without tourists. Larry and Jim Tull were having a chat.

"Don't call me Watson," said Larry, "And right now I don't think I would recognize peculiar if it was introduced."

"Okay." Tull grinned. "Danny and Phil searched the Blaney house. Guess what they didn't find."

"Didn't find? Jim, no games, okay?"

"They didn't find any guns." Jim Tull stood back and spread his hands. "They didn't find a single gun."

"Wait. No deer rifle?" Larry knew that everyone had a deer rifle and the town still had a butcher who knew how to dress a deer.

"Loaned it to a friend. Well, it's more like in hock. Doug gets – would have got -- his .303 back when he repaid a loan."

"So, were his guns stolen?" Tull started shaking his head.

"No, Larry, there never were any. Phil and Danny found lots of magazines, though: *Gun Digest*, *American Shooter*, *Shooter's Bible*, and they had all been read and re-read. Danny said there were notes in the margin, stuff underlined, notecards..."

"But why?"

Tull shrugged. "It was his hobby, Larry, and his passion." Tull unwrapped a cigar. He grinned. "His search for the most beautiful gun in the world."

"Oh, right. You've been working on that all day, I bet."

Tull spread his hands. "Larry, I call 'em as I sees 'em. And I got something else for you to consider."

"Okay. What?"

"The object in question is down at the police station with the other evidence we've collected, so let me describe it for you."

"Okay, Jim."

"It is a very well-done, well-printed brochure that describes certain facilities that a woman in difficulties might use."

"Are we talking about safe houses here?"

"Indeed we are, Larry. Very comfortable-looking, very safe-looking, safe houses."

"So Mildred was considering leaving Doug?"

"Maybe. There's a brochure anyway."

A thought occurred to Larry. "Is there a cost connected to this safe house? Because..."

"...Because Mildred couldn't afford it if there was a price. Right. So far as I can tell – and the secrecy here is amazing, I have no idea where this place even is

– but so far as I can tell, costs are picked up by government and by some interested groups."

"Groups like women's organizations."

"Exactly, Larry. And this brochure seems to have been given Mildred by a local representative of one, or perhaps, several of these groups." Tull grinned and rolled his cigar between his fingers.

"Wait," said Larry, "Not Rebecca Grant?"

"Yes, indeed. Ms. Grant wrote her phone number on the brochure for Mildred to call."

"Do you think Doug found out about this? You think that's why he stormed into the meeting."

"I think it's possible. But what I don't know is if Mildred was seriously thinking about leaving Doug and going to this place, or..."

"Or if Rebecca just dropped it off."

"Exactly."

"We have to talk to Rebecca again. And Mildred." Larry didn't quite sigh.

"Yep. Them's my feelings, too. Anyhow I made a call to Cantor, told him exactly what I wanted to know. He got back to me pretty fast. Said that Mildred had been thinking about this kind of place, but hadn't made up her mind whether or not to go." Tull looked at Larry and grinned. "Anyway, there's another place she said she preferred."

"Preferred? Another place."

"Yes. This other place is run by – wait for it – a religious group..."

"Janet Rimbert!"

"Exactly. Apparently this place was meant as a refuge for women escaping one of those Mormon breakaway groups, the ones that are polygamous."

"I can see that might..."

"Except that as soon as those women arrived, they left. Because of religion."

"Uh," said Larry.

"Doctrinal disputes. Theology. That's what they argued about. This group of evangelicals thinks Mormons are heretics, or something like that. They call it a 'funny religion', like Seventh Day Adventists and Jehovah's Witnesses. So they immediately began working to convert these women to the Way of Truth. And drove them away." Tull laughed. "You know, Larry, if they had just laid off for a few months, I bet half those women would have happy to join up, but..."

"Okay, Jim, so Janet Rimbert was talking to Mildred about leaving Doug, too."

"Right. They've got this refuge all set up and it's empty, so why not give Mildred a room."

"She didn't mention this when we asked her about where to stay."

"No," Jim agreed, "She called her cousin. Right away. Didn't mention either of these other options."

"And she didn't go home with either of them. I wonder if she suspects one of them killed her husband."

"Ah, now let's not get ahead of ourselves. We have to go back, ask Rimbert and Grant a few more questions."

24

Larry noticed some hubbub down the slope. Volunteers were putting the last touches on the stage by the lake. Four people stood in a group nearby, talking excitedly in loud voices, though Larry couldn't make out the words. Every now and then, someone would wave their arms about. "Jack and Marcy Stoneman, Jerry and Sandra Stoneman."

"Uh-oh," said Tull, "Looks like a Council of War."

Jack and Jerry Stoneman had been very successful realtors, back when there was property being bought and sold in Arcadia. Now, like everyone else, they schemed and scrambled. The Stoneman brothers usually had a deal or two cooking and once in a while they got involved in something that brought them a little cash. Jerry sat on Council and Jack was a power in the Chamber of Commerce and the Festival Committee.

Jim said, "Now they've seen us..." Sandra pointed up the rise of land toward Larry and Jim Tull, then the group turned and marched toward them. "Gang of Four," said Tull, "Going to re-educate us." He stuck the cigar in his mouth. He didn't fire it up, but held his lighter at the ready.

Jack and Jerry Stoneman were about a year and a half apart in age. They had played hockey on the same line when Arcadia had a Junior team going. Jack dropped out of high school at seventeen and went into the minors. Jerry followed him and sometimes played on the same line. Jack was twenty when he decided that there was no use pretending he might ever have a pro career. Jerry followed him out of hockey and into a realty company. Jerry always followed his brother. Even now, Jerry stood a little behind Jack, but he was an inch or so taller and could see over Jack's shoulder. Both Jack and Jerry drilled their gaze into Larry's face. On either side, their wives, Marcy and Sandra, gripped their mates' arms and glared. It was like a photo from a *National Geographic* article on primates.

"You!" said Marcy Stoneman.

Tull looked over his shoulder, then back. "You talking to me?" He grinned.

"Yes! Who do you think?"

"Well, now. What can I do for you?"

"You can do your damn job!" Marcy was yelling now. Pretty short fuse there, thought Larry.

"Well, I do my best..."

Jack Stoneman put his hand on Marcy's shoulder, she shrugged it off. "Now, Jim," said Jack, "What concerns us at this time is the impact the Blaney tragedy will have on LakeFest."

"I don't see that it should have any, Jack. It's not as though the murder is being discussed on the *National*. Not many reporters around. So I think..."

"No arrest yet," said Jerry. "Someone needs to answer for this crime. No matter how painful it may be, the guilty party needs to be arrested."

"I agree one hundred percent, Jerry. The guilty party needs to be arrested, tried, and punished. Yes, indeed." Tull nodded. "That is what needs to be done."

Jack pushed forward. "So why haven't you done it?"

Sandra laid a gentle hand on his arm. "We hear that you aren't going to arrest Mildred Blaney."

Bob Weber! thought Larry. Chatting with his associates in the business community.

Jerry moved in. "What's going on, Jim? We all know the problems at the Blaney household. A good lawyer will have her out in no time."

"Out?"

"Of prison! Goddammit!" Marcy was so angry she was spitting. The other three gave her some room. Jack didn't try to restrain her. She moved in on Tull and glared up into his face. "You going to do your job or not?"

"Of course, I'm going to do my job, Marcy." Tull grinned. "That's what I'm paid for."

The two couples moved in on Tull, Jerry Stoneman elbowing Larry to one side. They were all shouting at once. Jim Tull smiled at them, and lit his cigar. Thick clouds of smoke billowed around his head. "For god's sake!" Marcy backed up, waving the smoke away from her face.

Jack Stoneman recoiled from the smoke, but he didn't retreat, nor did Sandra Stoneman, still with her hand on Jack's arm. "Just tell us if an arrest is imminent, okay?"

"What I can tell you, Jack, is that we will make an arrest as soon as the evidence is clarified."

"It's pretty clear to us!" Marcy was still fired up.

"I see. Well, let's go down to the station and you can make a statement. Tell us what you know that makes this so clear."

"What?"

"Sure. I get your sworn statement on these events and what you know about them."

"Statement," repeated Jack. He backed away a little.

"*Sworn* statement, Jack." Tull puffed on his cigar. "From each of you."

"Well, now, Jim, I don't see that doing much good."

"No," said Jerry, "What good would that do?"

The four retreated a little, hovering on the edge of the cloud of cigar smoke that expanded around Jim Tull's head.

"Well, I don't know for sure, Jerry, but I think it might be useful to question anyone with knowledge of this crime." Tull pulled on his cigar, the cloud expanded, and the four moved a little further away.

"There's nothing we can tell you!" Jack said.

"Right," said Jerry. "Nothing!"

"What's wrong with you anyway?" Marcy began to cough and walked off. The others followed her.

"Now, what do you make of that?" Tull looked at his cigar. "Damn! This thing is hot."

"Maybe they were trying to find out what we know," said Larry.

"Hmm. Could be. They sure backed off when I suggested an interview."

"Yeah. Bob Weber was talking about arresting Mildred Blaney, too, but stopped when I asked him to make a statement." Larry paused. "I told him we had no plans to arrest Mildred. Sorry."

Tull shrugged. "Not a problem. Everyone can see we're not charging her. And I bet those women at the meeting know that she never left."

"So what are those four up to?"

"Hard to say. But, you know, looks a bit suspicious, doesn't it? Wonder which one of them organized this assault on local law enforcement."

"Jack appears to be the brains in that group."

"Jack wants to appear that way, but maybe somebody else is pulling his strings. How about Sandra? What do you make of her?"

"She was quiet the whole time."

"She's always quiet. She's one of those quiet ones, you look in their eyes and wheels are just clicking away. Stuff going on that they keep to themselves."

"One thing," said Larry, "If any of them know who killed Doug, I bet they wind up telling us."

"Yeah. Given the chance, any one of that group would sell out the others, either to make a nickel or to save their own skin."

25

Sometimes, in summer, a wave of cool air would roll down from the forest, fresh and full of oxygen, bringing relief from the heat for a few moments. Today the air was hot and thick and there was no breeze at all.

Anusheela sat with Larry up the grassy slope looking down onto the festival grounds. People were checking out the assigned places where they would set up their booths to try to make a few bucks. "Everybody here comes from somewhere else, I guess," she said. "Well, except you."

"Oh, I'm not from Arcadia."

"No, but from Canada, I think, and not very far away. Not another country, not even another province."

"Well, sometimes it seemed that way. My parents still spoke Russian sometimes and we were really separate from the larger community."

"You mean Canadians?"

"Yes. English, my mother called them. There was a lot of trouble at one point. Stuff being blown up and so on."

"Yes, I heard something about that. It was a long time ago though, right?"

"My father was growing up then."

"Really? Did he talk about it?"

"He told me about the D Squad. They were Ukrainian mounties sent to police the Doukhobors because they could understand Russian." Larry shook his head. "Sending Ukrainians to police Russians. It was crazy. They were taking the children away, then."

"Taking the children?" Anusheela was horrified. "Why?"

"Something about the schools. Some Doukhobors didn't want to send their children to Canadian schools, so the Mounties took them." Larry shook his head. "They said it was schools, anyway. I think it was just to break the community."

"I can't imagine... Your father? Was he..?"

"Yes. He said his mother hid him in a space under the pantry where they stored jam and pickles. The D Squad came in and searched. One of them had an iron bar, like a wrecking bar. He started thumping on the floor with it, listening for sounds that there were hollow spaces underneath. My father said that the bar broke right through the floor in front of his face. He yelled. They opened up the floor and took him."

"Oh, my. Was he in jail? I mean he was very young, wasn't he?"

"About twelve. They took him to New Denver, the same place where they kept Japanese during the War. There was a wire fence all around. His mother used to come and they would touch fingers through the wire."

"That's terrible." Anusheela was close to tears. "That poor woman."

"My father blamed her," said Larry. "He said if she had just sent him to school, then he wouldn't have spent all that time alone behind the wire."

"Oh," said Anusheela, "Oh, that's terrible."

"So, later on, after they let the children out of the camp, they arrested about four hundred Doukhobors and tried them for being arsonists and bombers. My father's father was one of them. They took them down to the Coast for that."

"So now he's lost both parents."

"Yes." Larry reflected that he had never thought of it that way before: his father, an emotional orphan. "There was a big march down to the Coast to see if they could get these men free. My father went with them. He was a young man by this time."

"Did they free them?"

"Some were freed. I don't know if it was the March to the Coast or the lack of evidence against them. My grandfather stayed in prison a few years. My father was camped outside the prison or in Vancouver most of that time." Where he learned to drink, thought Larry. "After grandfather was freed, my father brought him home. He died not long after – something wrong with his lungs – everyone said it was being in prison that made him sick."

"Your father went through a lot."

"Yes," said Larry, "He did." He decided not to mention what his father told him about being taken to the Leader's trailer, where the Leader pulled down his pants and introduced him to sex. Larry saw his father's face and recalled the tears running down his cheeks and his breath sharp with whiskey fumes as he sat on the edge of Larry's bed and choked out the shameful story.

"What on earth made you decide to become a policeman?"

"I wanted to help people. Police don't have to be D Squads."

"Police don't always help," said Anusheela.

"No. I learned that in Calgary, hustling junkies and Indians off the streets to places where people wouldn't have to see them. I was on the force there a few years and then I looked around for a better place to be a cop."

"It's not that bad here."

"No. And I have a lot more freedom in my job. I don't have to wear a gun unless I want to."

"Not much use for it here."

"No. I'll wear it during LakeFest though. The Americans expect it."

A crew shifted an ATM booth onto a concrete pad. The ATMs were chained down ever since some ex-millworkers had stolen one eight or nine festivals ago and driven away with it in a pickup truck. Larry had caught them down the road trying to open the ATM with a chainsaw. The ATM was still in the bed of the truck, so Larry made them drive it back to the festival grounds and put it back in place. Then he told the men to fuck off and not cause him any more trouble. The next year, the Festival Committee poured deep concrete pads with embedded iron rings to chain down the ATMs. These were permanent fixtures on the Festival grounds now.

The ATMs were contracted from private outfits who owned them. The companies charged transaction fees and paid rent on the pads to the Festival. Of course, the Festival Committee wanted Festival attendees to have access to as much cash as they could spend.

A man wrestled the ATM onto a dolly and wheeled it to the edge of the truck bed. Two other men guided the dolly onto a couple of boards serving as a make-shift ramp. This was an amateur crew compared to last year's. Probably just starting out, willing to pay higher rent for this opportunity.

It was hot under the sun and the three men were sweating and yelling at each other and swearing. Larry recognized the language. They were swearing in Russian. Then he noticed the men's tattoos.

"So they had cats tattooed on their arms," said Tull, "So what?"

"No, Jim. Winking cats wearing high hats, Russian prison tattoos. Jim, these guys are Russian crooks."

"Oh, Jesus! Just what we need." Tull wiped sweat from his face. "Okay, Larry, I trust your judgment on this." He sighed. "We'll have to call in the Mounties. I'll go back to the station, call somebody who'll refer me to somebody else who'll give me the runaround until I finally get the ear of whoever's in charge of Russian criminals. I'll give them the name of this outfit, too. They may already be known to the police, as they say."

Larry nodded. "Okay. I'll stay here. Whatever scheme they've got going won't start till the tourists get here, anyway."

"Day after tomorrow." Tull shook his head. "I'll get hold of Stoneman, too. Tell him there's not going to be any ATMs this year. But I'll talk to the RCMP first. In fact," Tull looked up at the sky, "In fact, I'll hold off telling Stoneman until tomorrow."

26

"Larry! What the hell is this?" Jerry and Jack Stoneman were shouting and waving their hands as they ran up the hill. It was a little after nine in the morning but the sun was already intense and sweat streamed down the men's red faces. They drew up in front of Larry, breathing hard.

"Well, we suspect some hanky-panky with the ATMs."

" 'Suspect'?" The Stonemans looked at each other. They weren't twins but it was easy to see that they were brothers; their dark comb overs were exactly alike. "What the hell do you mean 'suspect'? Is there a goddam problem or not, goddammit!"

"I think there is. We've called in..."

"Larry, we can't shut these guys down just because you get a wild hair up your ass!"

"I'm not saying that you should. We have some experts from the RCMP coming, just wait for them, okay?"

"Experts? Experts in what?"

"ATM fraud..."

"Oh, no. Oh, Jesus!" Jerry Stoneman turned on his brother. "I told you this would happen."

"Jerry, they were paying twenty-eight percent more. *Twenty-eight points*! We couldn't pass that up."

"Jack, you stupid..."

"Now don't you fucking start! I got my job, you got yours..."

"Yeah, you got your job! Hiring crooks and buying murder weapons!"

"You were the one that came up with those damn sticks!"

"Hold on," said Larry. He saw Jim Tull and two other men approaching. "Let's see what these men have to say."

One of the men with Tull was in uniform. He was short with Asian features. The man in plainclothes was huge, two hundred pounds at least, with hands thick as slabs of prime rib. Tull gestured over his shoulder. "Sergeant Shevchenko, Corporal Kobayashi. This is Officer Kalmakoff and Jack and Jerry Stoneman." Tull turned to the brothers. "We're just going to make certain about this but Shevchenko has brought a couple of warrants with him. He says he knows all about this bunch."

Everyone turned and stared at the big man in plain clothes. "Okay," said Tull, "Kobayashi is the tech who's going to examine this beast. There's the machine, Corporal." Everyone turned toward the short, uniformed officer. He grinned at them.

"Excuse me," said the big plainclothes officer as he squeezed past the Stonemans into the ATM booth. "Yeah," he said immediately. "Look here. See how the key pad is higher than it should be?" He pulled a small tool pouch out of his pocket and unzipped it. He selected an instrument and slipped the blade under the edge of the keypad and popped it up. Another keypad was underneath. "See, that's the original keypad. This thing on top records the keystrokes when you enter a PIN. And up here," He poked the card slot. "See how it sticks out? This is a reader. So your card and PIN numbers are recorded. Then they download this information and use it to print up a copy of your card."

"Shit!" said Jack and Jerry Stoneman, both at once.

"Yep," said Tull. "Gentlemen, I suggest you start locating an alternative to these machines which are going to be seized as evidence. Right, Sergeant?"

The short officer nodded. "That's right." The Stoneman brothers began yelling at each other. Shevchenko ignored them. "Now, where might we find the gentlemen who installed them?"

"They've got a tent behind the stage," said Larry.

The short officer smiled at him. "You're the guy that spotted the tattoos, aren't you?"

"Yes."

"Don Shevchenko."

"Larry Kalmakoff."

They shook hands and walked down the hill, Tull trailing behind them. "So," said Shevchenko, "You speak Russian?"

"Not really, but I understand it, or mostly do. My parents spoke it around the house."

"Yeah, I picked some up from my father. He was Ukrainian." He grinned at Larry. "Never learned any Japanese, though. My mother never spoke it."

"I see. Um, Corporal Kobayashi..?"

"His grandad was Japanese. Interned at the same camp as my mother's parents actually. You're Doukhobor."

"Yes."

"So how'd you know about the tattoos? I bet you never saw any of those in your family."

"No. It's just something I read about."

"Okay, then."

"That's their truck," said Larry. He pointed out the pickup that he had seen the men using the day before. A large canvas tent, about three meters across, stood nearby.

"Okay. Well, I think we just walk in the tent and bust these guys. I don't believe they'll put up much of a fuss but be ready just in case."

Larry was wearing his gun. He unsnapped the thumb break on his holster and Tull followed suit. "I'll just go in first," said Shevchenko. He pulled aside the canvas flap to reveal three cots side by side.

A man sat up suddenly and wiped his eyes. "Shit." His upper body was covered in tattoos.

"Hello, Yuri," Shevchenko grinned, "I'm happy to see you, too. In fact, I've got something in my pocket with your name on it."

"My name?"

"Yes. I figured you'd be involved here so I got the judge to issue a warrant just for you. Aren't you supposed to be at home now? That was a condition of your release, wasn't it?"

The men in the other two cots were sitting up now. They threw back their covers and a strong body smell rose in the tent. "Fuckin' *khuy*," one them muttered.

"Now, now," said Shevchenko, "None of that. I'm going to be nice and let you put on your pants before I arrest you. That's fair, isn't it?" Shevchenko pulled a pair of handcuffs from his belt.

27

"I can't drink while in uniform," said Shevchenko.

"Me neither," said Larry, "So I'll get Charley to open the back room for us."

Larry signalled to the bartender who nodded and pulled a set of keys from under the counter. Charley unlocked a door just off the barroom. "There you go," he said. "You want a pitcher?"

"Yeah," said Larry, "And something to snack on."

"Okay, I got wings and nachos."

"Both," said Larry.

They sat down at a long wooden table covered with scars and water rings from beer glasses. "This is pretty fancy," said Shevchenko. He gestured at the peacock tail patterned wallpaper. "Or at least it used to be."

"This was a private room for the silver kings back in the day when the mines were still going."

Charley brought in a pitcher of beer and glasses. Larry poured them each a glass. "Not often you see a Chinese bartender," said Shevchenko.

"Oh, Charley Mah owns the Century. Bought it years ago."

Charley brought in a platter of nachos and a tub of wings. "Okay?"

"Great, Charley. Thanks."

The two policemen sipped their beer in silence for a few minutes. After a while Shevchenko said, "That was a good call you made on those Russians. Lot easier to stop them before they start rather than clean up after they hit people's bank accounts."

"Yeah. What did that one guy call you? _Khuy_?"

"Means penis. He called me a prick."

"Huh. I never heard that particular word for penis before."

"It's bad guy talk. _Mat_, they call it. You don't hear it in polite society. It's like the tattoos, just belongs to them."

"I'll remember that." Larry resolved to look up more on the subject as soon as he could.

"So I hear you've got a murder case going."

"That's right." Larry stiffened. He wondered if the little Mountie was going to lecture him about solving murders. "Guy was beaten to death in his living room."

"Sounds domestic."

"His wife has an airtight alibi. It definitely wasn't her and I don't see her hiring anybody to do it.

But, wife or not, this was personal. The guy was battered over and over."

"Wife's boy friend, maybe? Girl friend?"

"None exists. Or none that I can find, anyway. Trouble is, this guy was really disliked." Larry shook his head. "Could have been just about anyone."

"And nobody is sorry that someone did it."

"Nobody except his wife, maybe."

Shevchenko shook his head. "That sounds like a tough one. Lots of cases like that never get cleared."

"Well, we're working on it."

"Sure. You've got a pretty good outfit here. Small, but on top of things. I bet this Festival business really stresses you though."

"We manage. There's auxiliaries, too."

"Oh, man, I hate working with auxiliaries." Shevchenko scooped up guacamole with a chip and dropped some jalapenos on it. "Anyway, you did pretty good today." He shoved the chip into his mouth. "You ever think about joining the Force?"

"No," said Larry, "I don't like horses."

Shevchenko laughed, shook his head. "Too bad. You're a good cop. Well, good luck to you."

Shevchenko stood up. "I have to head back, write this up." He grinned. "I better get somebody else to drive, though."

Larry finished off the beer and the nachos, wondering what kind of report Shevchenko was going to make about the Arcadia police. Well, nothing he could do about that. He got a take-out box from Charley and piled the leftover wings into it. He'd nuke them for supper.

28

Larry was polishing off the last of the wings and trying to get interested in a TV movie when Jim Tull knocked on his door. "Hate to bother you on your last free night, Larry, but... Mind if I come in?"

"No, Jim, come in. Sit down. Want a beer?"

"Thanks." He flopped on the couch and pointed at the television screen. "Don't want to spoil it for you, but the brunette is the one who did it. The man she killed knew stuff about her that she didn't want that numbnuts jock to find out. Because then he wouldn't marry her, see? Anyway, the blonde figures it out and almost gets killed, too, but the jock rescues her and they live happily ever after."

"Thanks for not spoiling it, Jim."

"That's all right. What're friends for, anyway?" Tull took a long pull on the beer bottle. "So, things went pretty well today."

"I guess. Did the Committee find somebody else to supply ATMs?"

"Yeah, they got the same outfit as last year. They won't be able to set up until the day after tomorrow and the Committee can't charge them as much as last time, so they are kind of unhappy with us."

"What? Jesus, Jim, we kept the tourists from being robbed blind."

"Sure, but some people say they wouldn't know it happened until after LakeFest was over, so it wouldn't matter."

"People would figure it out. It would hit the news and be a black mark against us in the future."

"That's what I told them, Larry. I expect they'll come around." Tull drank some more beer. "So how did you know about those tattoos?"

"Just something I picked up."

"Uh huh." Tull stared at him in silence.

"Well," said Larry, "I keep track of stuff like that." He walked over to a bookcase and pulled out a scrapbook. "Here's an article."

Tull took the scrapbook from him. "Clipped out of a magazine, eh? *Tattoo Life*?" Tull looked up at Larry. "You read this magazine all the time? You into tattoos, piercing, that kind of thing?"

"No. I read a lot of different magazines."

"Yeah, I see." Tull flipped through the scrapbook. *Psychology Today*: "Testing for Deviance". You think that works? Maybe we should test everyone in town."

"I don't know. I don't think that's a good idea."

"No. Probably they're all deviants. What's this? "Guide to Foreclosure"?"

"I was trying to find out if we could pressure the banks to take more responsibility for the empty houses in Dogpatch."

Tull looked up at him. "Son, here's some words of wisdom. In this country, we don't pressure banks ever. They run the show here and don't you forget it."

"Yeah, I came to that conclusion."

"Anyway, this book is very interesting. I'm glad you keep up with your studies here, Sherlock."

"Oh, man! The other day you called me Watson."

"You've been promoted. Sherlock Holmes kept a book like this, you know."

"Really?" Larry knew but he thought he'd let Jim Tull tell him all about it anyway.

"Yep. He did indeed. So, is there anything in this book of yours that will help us with our current homicide investigation?'

Larry shook his head. "I'm stumped."

"Me, too. And I doubt I can put any more time on it until after the damn festival is over." Tull put the scrapbook down on top of a pile of magazines on the coffee table. "So, let's take this last opportunity to go over this case." Tull paused. "You got another beer, by any chance?"

The two men re-hashed the case. Tull had brought the file with him and they re-read the autopsy report and examined the crime scene photos but could not come up with anything new. Larry said, "I went over the tapes some more."

"Better you than me," said Tull. "Find out anything?"

"No. I was looking to see who, besides Mildred, had a video alibi. You know, who was on camera the entire time or only off it for a few seconds."

"And?"

"And I got about four names. Three women from town and Aloe from Dolphin Starlight's place."

"You sound disappointed. Were you looking forward to interrogating her?"

Larry wiped a hand over his face. "Chrissake, Jim, what do you think..."

"Easy there, Larry. I kid, I kid."

"Okay. Look, among the ones without a video alibi, Janet Rimbert, Rebecca Grant, Marcy Stoneman were each missing for a period of time."

"Hm. Why them? Other than the fact that they are this town's – dare I say – heavy hitters among the women."

"Jesus, Jim, why do I bother?"

"Okay. Okay. Larry, I follow your reasoning – a little, anyway – Janet and Rebecca were both right there offering rides to Mildred and both showed up at the station later trying to defend her. Maybe one of them decided to defend her from Doug." Tull paused. "Or both?"

Larry shook his head. "There was only about five minutes when both were off camera at the same time."

"Right. Anyway, those two couldn't work together on anything without wrangling about it for hours first. Hard to see them teaming up in a murder. But it does look like they both were trying to get her to leave Doug. Why bother with that if you're going to kill him."

"Too rational, Jim. Doug Blaney was killed by someone who just lost it and whaled on him after he was dead. Someone may have started off with a plan, then gone haywire and lost it."

"Right. Okay, Larry. What about Marcy? She was doing the recording, wasn't she?"

"Yeah. She's not on camera at all except for the part where the women chase Blaney out of the church and then she just left the machine alone and joined the others. Nobody was behind the camera. It was on a tripod and just left pointing at one spot." Larry shrugged. "That's all I've got. It isn't much, I admit."

"No, no. This isn't that big a town. Every person eliminated is a step forward. If we had enough tape, we could eliminate everybody."

"There's a thought."

Tull laughed. He packed up the file and got ready to go. "So, any final thoughts, Sherlock?"

Larry shook his head. "Mildred has to be behind this somehow."

"Even if we didn't have that videotape, I'd doubt her as a killer. Can you really picture her beating somebody's head in?"

"No. But she's the one person everybody thought about when they heard Blaney was dead. She's the one with motive. She said it was her fault, too."

"She said what?"

"She said, 'It's all my fault.' When we interviewed her. I heard her."

"They all think it's their fault." Tull sighed and rubbed his eyes. "Every time they get beaten, these women figure it's because they did something wrong."

"Okay, I know about that but this seemed different the way she said it."

"How was that?"

"Oh, I don't know. I could barely hear her. Mildred hardly talks above a whisper at the best of times." Larry shook his head. "Forget it. I'm reaching. But Doug beating Mildred is the only motive I can see."

"So did she hire someone to kill Doug?"

"Hire with what?" Larry had gone over the Blaney's bank account. There had been no big withdrawals. In fact, the account had never held much more than a hundred dollars. There was no life insurance, either. And the Blaneys were behind in their mortgage payments; probably another foreclosure coming, eventually.

Larry said, "Maybe someone just wanted to help her."

"You mean, get rid of her abusive husband? Okay, but without Doug's unemployment cheques, Mildred has no income. Some help!"

"It's the best I've got, Jim. Maybe this good Samaritan just didn't think things through."

"Well, if it was a good Samaritan, he'll probably tell us about it. Those guys like to get the credit for their good deeds."

"So we wait for the confession."

Tull shrugged. "I got nothing."

"Me neither," said Larry.

So they left it there.

29

The sun rose into a cloudless sky and by nine o'clock the Festival area was radiating heat. People were busy setting up booths and tables; sweat ran down their faces and their hands were wet and slippery. Liz Honeycutt waved Larry over to her spot. She hadn't set up her booth yet. "Need a hand, Liz?"

"Not right now. No, a problem for you." Liz sighed, "Sorry, Larry, but I had some money stolen."

"What happened?"

"I was setting down my stuff. There was a box with some cash in it – a float so I can make change – about forty bucks."

"Okay. Did you see..?"

"Yes. I saw who it was. Looked up and saw him walk off with the box."

"Who?"

"Balbir. Nan's boy." Liz sighed again. "I am so sorry..."

"No. I'll go speak to him. Try and get the money back."

"Thanks, Larry. I appreciate it."

Balbir was behind the perogy tent, huddled against a trash can. The cash box was on his knees. The kid looked miserable. Larry shook his head and headed on over. He prepared himself for an attack, since he expected that kind of defense from a scared kid. But Balbir didn't say anything when Larry walked up and stood over him. "Balbir..?"

Balbir tried to look as defiant as possible but he didn't raise his head and there was a slight quaver in his speech. "Well, everybody else was making money so..." His voice trailed off.

Larry started to retort, "So you stole from a cripple?", but stopped himself. No use shaming the kid any more. Still, there was something that needed to be done. "Come on," he said softly, "Let's take that back to Liz."

"You do it." Balbir thrust the cash box straight up in the air as his head dropped lower.

"No," said Larry, "You have to do it."

Liz Honeycutt watched from her wheelchair as Larry and Balbir approached. Balbir stopped and Larry pushed him forward.

"Here," said Balbir in a small voice, and handed her the box. "I'm sorry."

"Yes," said Liz. "Well, I don't suppose we need formal charges and all but I still think some community service might be in order. Right, Officer?"

"Uh," said Larry.

"Exactly," said Liz. "Now, why don't you do some service by helping me set up this damn booth. I can't manage it alone."

Liz started giving Balbir instructions and he began assembling the frame that would hold the canvas that formed Liz Honeycutt's Festival store. Usually, she would have gotten assistance from the people who had set up on either side of her, but Larry realized that she had saved this chore for Balbir. He watched the two for a few minutes, then quietly left.

30

The crowd began forming pretty soon, people milling around the grounds, more and more of them. The tourists scouted out places for lunch, located the beer garden, and gaped at the lake and the mountains. The sun was unrelenting and the temperature climbed.

Marcy Stoneman set up her camera in front of some of the booths selling food and souvenirs. On the left, in the distance, was the stage with the lake visible behind it. Then, panning to the right, the crowd starting to find places on the grass that sloped down toward the stage. The good spots were filling up quickly. Past the crowd, still panning right, the beer parlor tent, already full at – Larry checked his watch – ten AM.

Larry noticed some action behind the canvas booths. Somebody was threading their way through the stacks of boxes and sacks of trash that were piled up there. Sandra Stoneman! She was creeping along, occasionally glancing toward the video camera. She was dodging the camera, thought Larry. Or she was dodging Marcy Stoneman. Now what was that all about? He walked over past the booths and intercepted Sandra.

"Great day, eh, Sandra?"

"What? Oh, yes. Yes. The weather's fine. Could be a little cooler." She smiled, hesitantly, then more broadly, as she began chattering about the weather and what it had been in years past.

Got a spiel all worked out, thought Larry, all she has to do is start reciting it. Wonder what's going on behind that smile? "You don't like to be on television, do you?" He grinned.

"Television? What?" Sandra started looking around.

"Well, you're dodging the camera." Larry gestured back toward Marcy Stoneman.

"Oh. Yes. I didn't want to spoil Marcy's shot." She turned on the full-beam smile again. "I thought I would just leave her be and not bother her." Sandra slipped on a pair of sunglasses. Larry thought, now I won't be able to watch the clicking wheels that Jim mentioned. Sandra looked behind Larry and waved. "I have to go. See Jack about..." Larry didn't catch her words as she walked over to Jack Stoneman who was hovering in the distance.

The two talked together for a few minutes, an intense but not excited conversation, no hand gestures, no arm-waving, then separated and walked off in different directions. So what was that all about? I used to think I knew this town, thought Larry, but I don't really know some people at all.

Larry walked back over to Marcy Stoneman and her camera. He looked out over the festival grounds, scanning from the booths to the lake to the stage. Sandra was right; it was a good shot.

Marcy didn't look up. "What do you want?"

Larry was taken aback. "Uh. Nothing, just wanted to know if you came up with anything new. That you remembered. From the meeting…"

"What the hell are you babbling about? I already told you I didn't see a thing that isn't on tape, so just piss off and let me do my job, okay?"

"Uh, okay." Larry walked off toward the booths. He thought, in future, maybe he'd leave Marcy's questioning to Jim Tull.

31

"Larry!" Jim Tull came up. "We got something."

Larry looked around at the crowd setting up their folding chairs near the stage. "Trouble already?"

"Not about the Fest. We found some bloody clothes and baby wipes."

"Baby wipes..."

"Yeah, like people use to wipe their baby's butt when they change diapers."

"Right, I saw some – a case, an unopened case – in the video of the meeting. Teeny Butt baby wipes, they were called."

"Yep," said Tull, "Teeny Butt baby wipes supplied by the manufacturers. They're organic and biodegradable, gluten-free and all that. The local drug store chain and the Teeny Butt boys worked a deal with the festival committee. Free baby wipes in exchange for publicity. Might even be a television commercial. People looking forward to their baby's butt appearing in that. Make their kid a star!"

"So what was found exactly?"

"Exactly what was found was a bunch of bloody baby wipes and a bloody jacket."

"Jacket?"

"Yeah. A small zip-up windbreaker kind of thing. Very light, very..." Jim paused and raised an eyebrow. "Very small."

"And no clue who it belongs to."

"Up until the meeting, it belonged to the Teeny Butt business people, but they presented it at the meeting. Maybe it was going to be a gift or something. Got the logo on it, baby butt and all." Jim Tull pulled out a cigar. "The jacket's made out of thin plastic or nylon. They passed it around at the meeting. Everyone oohed and aahed." Tull lit his cigar.

"So it's covered in fingerprints from everyone at the meeting."

"I expect so. It's on its way to a lab. We'll get a report in a month or two."

"So where was this jacket found, Jim?"

"Tourists found it. The ones parking at the Birdsong place." The tourists stayed in various campsites, usually, but these were a distance from the festival grounds. People who lived near the festival rented out their driveways and front yards as parking spaces to the tourists. "It was in the ditch by the road. Looks like someone bundled up the wipes in the jacket and pitched it."

"The Birdsongs live between the Blaneys and the Fountain of Blood."

"Sort of. The Blaneys are about three blocks past the Birdsongs – just a little too far to rent out their front yard, assuming they cleared out the junk that's piled up there now. You go the other way and you reach the festival grounds. But if you turn the corner at the Birdsongs, you head over to the church."

"Well, if someone was at the Blaneys and was going back to the church, they would turn right at that corner."

" 'Back' to the church?" asked Tull.

"Well, it keeps coming back to that meeting, doesn't it?"

"Maybe. Maybe we've just got that on the brain, just looking for tie-ins."

"Like the baby wipes. And the jacket."

"Yes. Like that."

A thought struck Larry. "How'd the tourists take it?"

"Oh, they're all right, I think. They've parked at the Birdsong house before. Lou and Cindy do everything they can to keep them happy. I think Cindy baked up a bunch of cookies or something for them."

"How much do the Birdsongs charge?"

"Eighty dollars a day. Lou was talking about lowering it to seventy-five for people who booked in advance with a deposit, like these regulars, but other parking people are talking about raising the rent." Tull drew on his cigar. "Group got together, wanted to form a Parking Association, set the same fees for everyone so as to end any competition."

"Right."

Tull went on. "They met, talked about what the traffic would bear and how high they could boost the rent. Someone suggested that they get an ace negotiator to do the dirty work and talk to the prospective parkers."

"Don't tell me!"

"Yes, that person was Jack Stoneman. He only wanted to charge a flat ten percent for his services."

"Ten percent!"

"Yeah. I figure Stoneman would have gone down to eight, maybe even five, but nobody wanted to negotiate. The Birdsongs, for instance, thought Stoneman was just another leech begging forty or fifty hard-earned dollars from their piggy bank." Tull shook his head. "Stoneman never had a chance."

32

Larry walked toward the Safe Mothers tent. He was hoping to find Rebecca Grant without having to enter the Safe Mothers area and pass through whatever security or visitor regulations they might have for men. And, as luck would have it, there she was, exiting the women-only zone. "Rebecca?"

"What is it, Larry? I'm busy."

"Yes, Rebecca, I know." We're all busy, he thought. "I just wanted to ask you about a leaflet that we found in the Blaney house."

"Leaflet? What?"

"You wrote your telephone number on it."

"So what? Is it illegal for women to call each other?"

"What we were wondering is if Doug saw the leaflet." Rebecca paused, waiting. "We're thinking maybe that's what set him off."

"Okay. You're talking about a brochure for Northern Womyn's Safe Place, right?"

"Yes. That's what I'm asking about."

Rebecca started to snap something back, then stopped, and looked away. "I never thought of that. That Doug might have found the brochure. I was trying to help Mildred."

"Sure," said Larry. "But Doug..."

"Yeah, Doug!" Rebecca clenched her jaw so hard Larry thought she might chip a tooth. "Well, I never thought he would even see the brochure, but I guess he searched Mildred's stuff."

"Could be," said Larry. He knew the brochure had been found on a coffee table on top of a stack of shooting magazines.

"I hate to think that's what caused this." Rebecca looked off, then rounded on Larry. "But he was responsible! He was the one beating his wife! He..!. He..." Rebecca ran out of gas.

"Okay," said Larry, Doug Blaney was a wife-beater."

"Right!" said Rebecca.

"And a murder victim." Larry paused. "Whether he deserved it or not – and there's probably not many people in town who would say he didn't..."

"Not many?" Rebecca made a sarcastic face.

"Okay, probably just about everyone thinks Doug deserved this," Larry paused, "Except Mildred."

Rebecca put her hands to her face. "Oh, God! Some women get so twisted..."

"So, do you think Mildred was going to go to your retreat?'

"Safe place!"

"Yes. Safe space. Place."

"No. I think she was going to some place that Janet Rimbert suggested. Some religious thing." Rebecca waved a hand in the air. "Probably she'll have to wear a red uniform and recite scripture all day."

Larry was confused. "Red uniform?"

"Like Gilead." Rebecca glared at him. "Never heard about *The Handmaid's Tale*?"

"Oh, right. Yes. I guess that is a uniform, isn't it?"

Rebecca gave a disgusted look and waved off Larry's words. "Listen. I respect Janet Rimbert. She has deep-felt beliefs and I respect that. And she doesn't let her husband push her around, she tells that jerk where to get off." Rebecca smiled, reminiscing about some incident or other. "Anyway, if that's what Mildred wanted, I have to accept it."

Those last words were almost choked out and Larry wondered just how much Rebecca could accept. But before he could ask any more questions, she flapped a hand at him and walked away.

33

About three o'clock the first warm-up acts took the side stages. Amateurs, kids that had just formed a group, a bar band or two from as far as three hundred miles away. Around five, the heat let up a little and the temperature gradually descended to a livable level. The main acts took the stage around nine o'clock – once-famous groups mostly, now playing their hits. This first day featured no one that Larry remembered, but since

Lakefest began, his interest in music had waned. Now he associated certain songs with moods and events that he had gone through over the years.

The first day wasn't the worst, usually, just finding lost kids, getting tourists with heatstroke to the Aid tent, and so on. Later in the week was when the nasty drunks started fighting and there were thefts, sometimes pickpockets, hard drugs. Even so, at the end of the first, easy day, Larry collapsed into bed around one thirty, exhausted.

The phone woke Larry from a deep, dreamless sleep. "Yeah," he mumbled.

"Larry, I hate to do this to you." It was Plaskowitz.

Larry sighed. "Tell me, Phil."

"Well, somebody tried to burn down a house in Dogpatch."

"What!"

"Yeah, there's gasoline and candles and stuff. I saw a candle through a window when I was doing a round up here."

"Okay, Phil, give me an address."

Larry went to the closet for his uniform, then realized he was wearing it. He splashed cold water on his face and drove up to Dogpatch. It was four in the morning. He'd had two and a half hours sleep.

The town fire truck was spinning its blue light and the crew were shining spotlights here and there. The volunteer fire fighters lounged around, yawning. The excitement of being called out had waned and they wanted to go back to bed; most of them would be working all day at the festival.

Larry walked into the house and down the basement stairs. The place reeked of gas fumes. And there it was: big cans of gasoline, a puddle on the floor, a couple of candles that someone had lit, apparently meaning them to burn down and ignite the gas. Larry eyed the cans and wondered if they could get any prints from them. Probably not -- gasoline was a pretty good solvent -- but they would try. The candles were ordinary white emergency candles. There were boxes of them in the hardware store, the grocery store, the drug store... And everyone bought them all the time since there were always power outages during the summer thunderstorm season or when winter ice took out a line.

Who would do such a thing? Who would try to burn down Dogpatch?

Plaskowitz appeared at Larry's elbow. "Phil? Who used to live here?"

"Oh, let's see. I think their name was Bergeron, something like that. But they haven't lived here in maybe ten years."

"I guess the bank owns this place, then."

"Well, actually, I think somebody bought it."

"Bought it?" Bought a house in Dogpatch?

"Yeah, Larry, a company, I think. I'll try to find out in a couple of hours."

"Good." Larry started to turn away. "Phil," he said, "This was good work."

"Uh, gee. Thanks, Larry."

"How'd you spot it anyway?"

"There was a little bit of flicker from the candle. There was stuff taped around the windows, but the tape didn't hold and a corner came loose. So I came up to the house and looked in and saw the candles and called the fire department."

Plaskowitz was pale and thin and his hair stuck up when he took his hat off. He wore big, thick glasses and everyone thought he was probably half-blind. Have to revise that assessment, thought Larry, and the one about him being stupid, too. He just looked that way. "Anyway, good police work, This could have been really bad. You might have saved some lives here."

"That's great. I mean, that the lives were saved and all. Uh, Larry?"

"Yes?"

"The chief said I should tell you to go back to bed and not worry about this. He said he'd look into it with me and that Lakefest should be the only thing on your mind tomorrow." He looked down. "I'm sorry I woke you up."

Larry nodded. "No problem, Phil. But you can call me anytime. This was good work." He thought another couple of hours sleep sounded mighty good. He drove back home. This time Larry managed to get out of his uniform, but his mind kept turning over the night's events. Who would set a fire in Dogpatch? He was just beginning to drop off when his alarm sounded.

34

Larry's head snapped up. He had been dozing. A plate of eggs and bacon and sausage stared up from the table at him. "Larry? You okay?" Anusheela hovered beside him.

"Yeah. Just grabbing a nap, that's all."

"Yes." Anusheela looked over at another table where a bunch of tourists were gesturing at her. "Well, it's almost hump day. Soon be over." She hustled over to the tourists' table and gave them a smile.

Hump Day! That was tomorrow. The Fest would only be half over and he still had today to reckon with. Larry forced himself to eat his breakfast. He knew he needed it but all he wanted to do was sleep.

Around noon, as Larry was walking past the beer garden, his eyes suddenly blurred and he felt like he was going to pass out. He managed to get down to Liz Honeycutt's booth and walked around back and sat on the grass.

"She said it was okay. She said for me to look after things." Balbir looked down at Larry. He was alone in the booth.

"It's all right, Balbir. I just needed a place to... to..." Larry bent forward, head on his knees. Everything looked white, whether his eyes were open or closed. Suddenly, he felt a trickle of cold running down his spine. "What?"

"Liz... Ms. Honeycutt, keeps this cloth in a bucket of ice water for people that have too much sun." Balbir paused. "I'm sorry I got your uniform wet."

"It'll dry. Hit me with that ice water again, Balbir. It feels good."

Balbir put the cloth on the back of Larry's head again. "Ms. Honeycutt says that next year I should take the first aid course so that I can be a helper at the festival. Perhaps you should take a salt tablet now."

"Good idea. And put some of that ice right on top of my head. Okay? Thanks, Balbir, I owe you for this."

"That's okay, um, um..."

"Larry."

"Yes. Larry." Balbir paused. "You should lie down now."

Oh, God, thought Larry. Is Balbir going to be my nurse now? This is what marriage must be like, always someone telling you to be careful, to take care of yourself, to... Larry's head snapped erect. "What?"

"I didn't say anything."

"No. No. I must have drifted off." Larry scrambled to his feet.

"You need sleep," said Balbir.

"Yes, I know." Larry walked back out into the heat.

Larry spotted Janet Rimbert far down the concourse between the booths, walking his way. Well, he thought, that's convenient. Larry was standing by the Honey Man booth run by Herb Macklin. Herb had a few hives and put up honey all season to sell at LakeFest. There was a tray of honey and sesame treats covered with plastic wrap to keep away the insects. Herb gave the treats to people passing by in hopes that would get them to buy his honey. Now Herb picked up the tray and put it under the counter.

Janet Rimbert kept coming toward Larry and he noticed a flurry of apprehension among the people working the booths. Both hands on the counter, Tim Talbot the T-shirt maker watched Janet approach. Tim made paper pre-prints of his designs, then used a heat press to transfer them onto shirts. He left off the dates, which were pressed onto the shirts as they were purchased. Left-over shirts could be sold at the next LakeFest. Or the one after.

Janet walked straight up to Tim and Larry decided to join them.

"Not this year, Janet. Everything is fine," said Tim.

"Now, Tim, I know and you know that we are all human and we all make mistakes." Janet bit her lower lip. "Sometimes, we make big ones."

Tim shook his head. "Nope. Not this year. Every shirt is perfect." Tim paused. "So far. Knock on wood." He rapped his counter.

A disgusted look crossed Janet's face. "Sure, Tim. I understand." She turned on her heel and walked into Larry.

"Whoops! Sorry, Janet."

Janet glared at Larry for a moment. "What do you want?"

"I do have a question or two. Say, what's going on with Tim?"

"Sometimes he messes up the printing and there are shirts that can be rescued from the trash heap."

In fact, Larry knew the shirts didn't need rescuing. Half the kids in town wore Tim's mistakes, but not during LakeFest because Tim thought it was poor advertising. "I see. Well, I wanted to ask you about the place you found for Mildred Blaney. The safe house."

Janet shrugged. "I thought she was going to go, but she decided otherwise, I guess." A smile flickered around her lips. "She doesn't need it now." Janet paused before adding, "Praise Jesus."

"Okay. What I want to know is whether Doug knew about this."

"I guess so!" Janet looked at Larry. "That's why he came charging into the meeting."

"You're sure about that, Janet? Doug was upset that Mildred might be leaving and..."

Janet flapped a hand in the air. "Looks that way. But you're the detective, you tell me." She gave a little sneer and stalked off.

At least she didn't pray at me, or curse me, or whatever she was doing back at the police station, Larry thought. Janet seemed quite settled now.

"Every year," said Tim.

"What?"

"Every year she comes around and wants free shirts. You know, I get a couple of bucks from people for the seconds. Not much, just enough to make up some of the cost. But, the Rimberts..." Tim shook his head. "Pete says write it off as a donation to the church. Write it off of what! It's not like I have any income to speak of. Then Janet says, my reward will come from Jesus, if I only prepare and believe and pray and," Tim took a breath, "And give her a bunch of T-shirts."

"I saw Herb hide the honey treats."

"Yeah, everyone with freebies has to watch out for the Rimberts." Tim shook his head. "I mean, all the freebies we offer, to try to get customers in, all the freebies cost us something and everybody knows that and no one goes around ripping off the freebies. Except the Rimberts. Fuck 'em."

"Okay, Tim." Larry was a little worried that the man was getting over-excited. Tim was a big man and scary when he was angry. "Now, smile, before you frighten the tourists."

Tim smoldered a second, then burst into laughter. "Okay, Larry. I'll be a happy boy! Okay?"

"Sure," Larry grinned. Tim was a pretty good guy. He did have a temper, but it didn't last long. Long enough to beat a man's head in, thought Larry, then shook his head. Everyone's a suspect, he thought, every single person in town. Everyone except Mildred Blaney.

35

Tull leaned back in his chair and stuck a cigar into the middle of a huge grin.

Larry fell into a chair next to the desk. "What are you so happy about?" It was almost midnight and he was exhausted. He rubbed his sunburned neck.

Tull said, "Well, Sherlock, we have a lead in the Blaney murder."

Larry sat up and took notice. Tull lit his cigar. He took his time about it, carefully rotating the cigar between his lips and puffing until a huge cloud of smoke rose around his head. Larry said, "Are you going to tell me or can I take a nap?" He waved smoke away from his face.

"Now don't get snippy. I got a call from that mountie, Corporal Shevchenko. Remember?"

"Sure. It was only a couple of days ago. Or a week or something." Larry shook his head. "What did he have to say?"

"First of all, he sends you his regards. You made quite an impression on him, Sherlock." Tull sucked on his cigar and slowly let a cloud of smoke rise from his mouth. Larry kept quiet. "Anyway, what the good Corporal had to say was that they found a link between our town and the Russkis."

"A link?"

"A local person, a member of this community."

"Well, Jack Stoneman hired them."

"Right! But how did our esteemed C of C president know about them in the first place?" Tull drew on his cigar and waited for Larry to respond.

"Jim? Can we get on with it? Before I cram that stogie lit end first right up your..."

Tull shook his head. "Tsk, tsk. All right, I'll tell you. He heard about the Russians through our local contact for the Hell's Angels."

"What? The Hell's Angels?"

"Well, actually their satellite club up in Revelstoke."

"Who are we talking about? And Revelstoke's pretty far away. Anyway, I haven't seen a biker in town for years."

"Revelstoke isn't so far that a local with a business opportunity can't get up there."

"Business opportunity?"

"Yep, turning abandoned houses into grow-ops. This was before legalization. That was the plan. Some of the bikers came down for a visit but they canned the idea."

"We'd shut them down in a minute!"

Tull raised an eyebrow. "Some of that going on already. Small scale, though." Several of the families still living in Dogpatch raised a little marijuana for personal use and to supplement their income. The stuff was legal now but there were rules about selling it. The police left them alone. But any house with a grow-op in it would not be covered by fire insurance, not that anyone in Dogpatch bothered with insurance any more.

"Real grow ops would stick out like a sore thumb," said Larry. "I mean new ones. Not what Sullivan and the Kroetsch family and some others have in their basements -- those are maybe a dozen plants each. An entire house turned into a grow op is a different matter. And even a small increase in traffic would stick out in Dogpatch."

"Sure. There's too many empty places. A little activity would be very noticeable."

"Okay, the bikers say No. So the Russkis were looking at grow-ops?"

"Nope. By the way, you can probably guess who the local contact was."

Larry thought for a moment. "Doug Blaney."

"Exactly, Sherlock, Doug Blaney. Or, as a confidential source told our Corporal Shevchenko, 'a half-assed gun freak looking to get busted'."

"Okay," said Larry, "I got it. Now get to the Russians."

"All right." Tull chuckled, "There's another piece to the puzzle, though. Another local also saw a business opportunity and used his real estate connections to pick up some property."

"Not Jack Stoneman."

"Both the Stonemans, actually. They saw all that property going cheap at foreclosure auctions and decided it would make a good investment."

"Investment? As a grow-op?"

"Well, they'd probably deny any connection to drugs but I suspect they saw an opportunity. Anyhow, Blaney introduced them to the bikers, who introduced them to a crooked lawyer they know, who contacted the Stonemans and helped them set up a company." Tull picked up a paper and waved it. "Here's the official paper. A numbered company. The lawyer's office is the registered address and the officers of this company are: Jack Stoneman's wife Marcy, Jerry's wife Sandra, and Mildred Blaney."

"Jesus!" Larry sat back. "That wouldn't really protect them legally."

Tull shrugged. "Who knows what those wheeler-dealers were thinking. So they put together a company to invest in local real estate."

Larry thought, Get to the point! "Investment? Who would want to invest here?"

Tull laughed. "Slow down, Cowboy. The idea was to get a piece or two of decent property in upscale areas, maybe on the Coast or in the Okanagan. These would disguise all the unsalable stuff from here. See, they lumped all the property together, then sold shares in the complete package. They could point to the good property and give the buyer to understand that was typical. They got the idea from the big financial disaster of 2008. You put all the garbage together, sell people a tranche..."

"A tranche?"

"A slice of the whole package, a share. So you got two properties valued at, say, a million each and forty-eight properties at ten thousand each. That's almost two and a half million. Then you get people to buy in at ten thousand a share, you sell three hundred shares, three million bucks, you've made more than a half million dollars. Or at least that's the way it was supposed to work."

"I'm already guessing that this isn't legal."

"Maybe not. Depends on what the investors are told, I'd say."

"Anyway, it didn't work."

"Nope. The Stonemans never could pick up a piece of good property to disguise the crap. And they never got a single investor, either."

"So they wound up with forty-eight houses in Dogpatch."

"Just three, actually, then they ran out of capital. Or credit. Not much cash involved, I think, all imaginary money." Tull puffed on his cigar. "So through the lawyer they came in contact with the Russians. Maybe the Stonemans thought their plan would make a good money-laundering scheme. Instead, they wound up giving the Russians the ATM contract."

"You know, these are not the brightest criminals I ever heard of."

"No. Anyway, Doug Blaney was always claiming to be an expert on crime and stuff, so he had some feelers out, hinting at money-laundering operations involving real estate."

"Aha!"

"Yeah, something else he took to the bikers as a proposal. But that was for the lawyer to arrange, probably, which would be the moment, I think, that Blaney would discover he was no longer part of the scheme"

"Wait! You don't mean he was killed because..?"

Jim Tull blew a smoke ring. "No, no. There was never any big scheme to protect. But once Blaney brought these people together, then he had no more part to play. You bet they would cut him out of the deal once there was money to be made. Anyway," Tull waved his cigar. "The bikers themselves just looked at buildings for grow ops. They weren't really into tranches or anything like that. So the bikers backed off and the investment didn't fly and I guess that's when the Stonemans decided to scam the insurance company. Of course the fact that the only insured houses in town were the ones to burn wouldn't bother the insurance companies. No sir."

"Jesus! You mean they set that fire last night?"

"Well, looks like they tried to set it, but failed, thanks to some ace police work."

"I already told Plaskowitz that he did a good job."

"Yeah, he's all puffed up about it. People know you tell the truth, Larry." Tull sucked on his cigar. "Anyway, the Stonemans got pretty desperate."

"They're lucky they didn't wind up in a shallow grave, considering who they'd been trying to work with."

"Yeah, bikers and Russians."

"Okay," said Larry, "You've just added a few hundred suspects to the Blaney murder."

"Oh, I believe we should think locally, Sherlock."

Larry nodded. "The Stonemans."

"Yes." Tull puffed on his cigar. "You know, it's going to be fun telling City Council that one of their esteemed members is an evil crook. That'll be right after I tell them about the great police force they are paying for and how a smart cop managed to avert disaster." Tull grinned. Larry could see his teeth shining through a cloud of cigar smoke.

"Right," said Tull. "Now go home and get some sleep. Tomorrow morning -- or this morning, depending on how you look at it..."

"Jim, you're babbling."

"Right. Okay. In a few hours, while the Stonemans are fiddling the LakeFest books, we'll go have a chat with them."

36

Jim Tull and Mayor Wolichuk were having a conversation near the beer garden when Larry arrived. The mayor looked at Larry and intoned, "The foxes have flown from the hencoop."

Larry said. "Uh..." and looked at Tull.

"They're gone, Larry. Jack and Jerry Stoneman and their wives. Also, there seems to be a pile of Festival money missing." Tull's eyes twinkled and Larry thought the Chief might be stifling a laugh.

"How much is missing?"

"Well, that is a topic to be considered by experts", said the Mayor. "I have an accountant coming over to look at the books and give us a considered opinion."

Larry turned to Tull. "Now what?"

"Well, RCMP and local forces around the province and into Alberta have been alerted. There's a lookout at the various airports and the border." Tull grinned. "Good descriptions complete with license plate numbers are circulating. And we have their credit card info so..."

Larry said, "You think they might hook up with the bikers?"

"Bikers?" squeaked the mayor.

"If they do contact a motorcycle club, I expect that group of good citizens will turn them in right away. Anyhow, it was Blaney who was the biker contact."

"Blaney? Doug Blaney?"

"Yes, Your Worship. The dear departed." Tull turned back to Larry. "The Russians might turn them in as well. Or..." Tull shrugged.

"Russians..." Wolichuk looked as though he might collapse.

"Don't worry, Your Worship. It's all sorted out." Tull paused. "Well, pretty much, anyway. And, look, yonder approaches your expertise!"

Charley Gilmore, bank manager, hustled up to the group. Wolichuk briefly explained the situation and the two left to interrogate the festival computer.

"You know, Larry, our mayor is not so stupid. Charley there is one of the few local accountant-type people who has no connection to the Stonemans. Also, he handles the Festival account, which apparently the Stonemans couldn't get into. All that they got was one day's worth of cash and, since most folks get their tickets in advance, that ain't much. Mostly they got a day's worth of beer garden takings, which of course, is not inconsiderable."

"So where does that leave the Blaney murder?"

"Get right to it, don't you, Sherlock? Well, that is a different kettle of fish to fry, as His Worship might say." Tull unwrapped a cigar. "I'd say it leaves us exactly where we were."

"But we weren't anywhere. I mean... Unless Marcy Stoneman..."

Precisely, Sherlock. We still aren't anywhere." Tull dragged on his cigar. "And I don't have any evidence that Marcy is a murderer. So..."

"So back to policing the festival."

"Right. How you holding up anyway?"

"Not bad. And today is Hump Day."

Tull stared at Larry and puffed on his cigar.

"Whatever keeps you going, Larry. Whatever."

37

There were fewer Fest-A-Rods in evidence today than the day before. In fact, many of the festival auxiliaries had left the sticks at home on the first day of LakeFest. It was just too creepy, carrying around a murder weapon. And suppose you had to use one? Would that make you a murder suspect? Anyway, there hadn't been a problem with the Fest-A-Rods and for that, Larry was grateful. People wearing the Auxiliary armband had both hands free to direct tourists to the aid tent or the lost children shelter or the beer garden.

Then Larry caught sight of Pete and Janet Rimbert bearing down on him, each clutching a Fest-A-Rod. Here comes trouble, Larry thought, and placed himself in a bit of shade near the pulled pork trailer. Pete was still twenty feet away when he opened up. Larry missed the opening salvo but heard Pete yell, "What are you going to do about it?"

"I didn't catch that, Pete. Do about what?"

"The...the...Rods!" Pete sputtered.

Janet took up a position at Pete's shoulder. "Are you incompetents capable of getting anything right?"

"What about the Rods? Aren't there enough? Because that's out of my..."

"No, you..!" And then they both started yelling and calling him names. They were red-faced and sweating and Larry turned his body so as to keep them in the sun facing him while he remained in the shade.

"Now, Pete, Janet, don't everybody talk at once, I can't hear what you're saying."

"You hear what you want to," sneered Janet. And Pete joined in and they were yelling again.

Larry took off his hat and slowly fanned his face until the Rimberts exhausted themselves. "Rods?" he asked, helpfully.

Pete was gasping for lack of breath. Larry thought the man might have a heart attack. He felt a little guilty about hogging all the shade, but that feeling quickly passed. Janet took up the slack. "No one is carrying their rods!" She brandished a Fest-A-Rod in

Larry's face. For a moment Larry thought she was going to hit him with it.

Pete nodded, "No one! They're just...just...naked!"

Larry thought, Well, if they were naked and carrying their rods, then I'd have to arrest them. But then, if they hid their rods, perhaps they wouldn't be naked. Lord! he thought, I've been hanging out with Tull and the Mayor too long. He held up a hand. "So the problem is that the auxiliaries aren't carrying Fest-A-Rods?"

"That's what we've been saying for the last ten minutes," snarled Janet.

"This is not just protection," said Pete, "This is a Business Opportunity!"

"So this town can make enough to pay all the public salaries to those who take from those who make!" Janet eyed Larry up and down, pausing when her gaze got to his badge.

"I see," said Larry. "Well, you know that seems to me to be a responsibility of the Festival Committee. I actually have no authority over how the auxiliaries are outfitted."

"Nobody seems to be able to find Jack Stoneman," said Janet.

"Probably sleeping it off somewhere after that ATM mess," said Pete.

"But, Janet," said Larry, "Aren't you on the committee? Shouldn't it be you who..."

"No one's listening to me! Including you!"

"What about, oh, Mr. Starlight?"

"His job was to train the auxiliaries! That's all!" Janet was screaming now.

"Well, even so. I suppose you could try to withhold some of what you're going to pay him. Might be an incentive..."

"He was paid in advance. Against my advice." Pete glanced at Janet and lifted his chin in triumph.

"Oh, shut up! Who needs your advice?" She snapped back at her husband. For a moment, Larry thought small, wiry Janet and big, sinewy Pete might start swinging. But then they drew back from facing each other and glared at Larry.

"Now look at this mess!" Pete was breathing heavily again. "But you aren't going to do anything, are you?"

"Well, Pete, I don't see that this is within my authorized duties. No, I'm not going to do anything." Larry smiled as he watched the couple walk away, arguing with each other.

"Larry!" Bob Weber ran up breathless, anxious to speak.

"Oh. Bob." Larry's smile broadened. "How's business?"

Weber choked. "Uh, great, great." He collected himself. "But I hear there are serious problems." He gave Larry a significant look and began nodding his head. "Serious," he intoned.

"What kind of problems, Bob?" Apart from Russian gangsters, attempted arson, absconding thieves, and – not to forget – a murder, thought Larry. "Problems, Bob?"

"Well, I'm talking about the theft of all the proceedings of the Festival." Weber shook his head. "Be a big blow to the community, a big blow."

"Oh. From what I hear, it's not that terrible. But the accountant is looking into it now and we'll have the final word pretty soon."

"That's wonderful, Larry, just wonderful." Weber's eyes lit up.

"Yes, it is, Bob." Now you have a rumor to spread, Larry thought, and maybe it will help people feel like they aren't suffering through a complete disaster here.

"Great, great! But of course we do have the loss of once-trusted members of the business community."

"I can't comment on that, Bob."

"No, no, of course you can't. Still..."

"But you know what they say."

"Terrible loss, terrible... What?"

"What?" said Larry.

"What do they say?"

"Oh. They say that crisis is another word for opportunity. Actually, they say it's the same word."

"Who says?"

"The Chinese. See, in Chinese, the same word means both crisis and opportunity." Larry paused watching Weber's eyes jumping around in his round face. "Of course, I don't speak Chinese, so maybe it's all nonsense. Still, it's something I heard from a businessman once."

"Really?"

"Yes, he had it printed on a little card that he handed out."

"What business was he in, Larry?"

"Investments, Bob, investments." Larry paused. "He should be out soon. His sentence was only fifteen years." Lord forgive me for messing with this poor man, Larry thought.

"What? Prison? What?"

"He was a criminal." But I just can't help it. "But, Bob, we should look to the truth of his statement rather than the sad result of his actions."

"Uh."

"For instance, I see opportunity as the business community re-news its leadership. The Chamber of Commerce will need a new president, for example. Some dynamic person who can re-energize that group."

"Of course," said Weber. His eyes flickered from the right to the left and back again so quickly that it looked to Larry as though they might have rotated in his skull. "Yes, yes. And that's what business is all about. Creative destruction, they call it. Yes."

Oh, Lord, thought Larry, I should have known better. Jim Tull is right. I shouldn't try to be anything but straight-forward with people. "Well, Jack Stoneman was destructive, I guess, and other people will now be creative."

"Yes!" said Weber. "Of course, we're sort of doing it backwards."

Creative destruction backwards is destructive creativity, thought Larry. His eyes drifted toward the abandoned mill site down the lake. When he looked back, Bob Weber was a few booths away, talking to everyone, waving his arms about. Campaigning, thought Larry, as he watched Weber carom from one person to another and down the row of booths like a rubber ball. Larry was tired and numb from exhaustion, otherwise he would have felt more guilty than he did.

All in all, Hump Day wasn't so bad. Only one more day to go before the last day, thought Larry as he collapsed into bed at 2 A.M. "Almost over," he said, and Anusheela kissed him on the forehead at the beginning of a dream that he didn't remember in the morning.

38

"Almost over," he said to Anusheela, as she dropped a plate of eggs and sausage and toast in front of him. She gave him a distracted smile and ran over to a table of clamoring tourists.

"Almost over," he said to Liz Honeycutt. She nodded, non-committal behind her jewellery display. Behind her, Balbir jumped up. "Over?" He looked worried.

"Tomorrow's the last day."

"Oh," said Balbir.

"Don't worry, Balbir. It'll be back next year." And the year after and the one after... Larry suddenly saw an endless procession of LakeFests before him, stretching past the horizon. He stopped smiling.

"You all right, Larry?" Liz examined his face. She looked back down at her jewellery. "I think of this as Crazy Day. This is when it starts to get to people – the heat, lack of sleep. Some folks hallucinate. Happened to someone that had a booth next to mine one year. He just went round the bend."

"What happened?" said Balbir, eyes wide.

"Well, he started talking to himself, or someone no one else could see, louder and louder. Then he took off all his clothes and sat in front of his booth, singing."

"Singing?"

"Yeah. Golden oldies, I guess, except when he changed the lyrics into jokes. So he sang 'The hills are alive, with the sound of mucous' and 'I want to hold your gland'. Like that." Balbir stared, mouth open. He'd never heard of these songs. "And he'd sing dirty versions," Liz sighed. "Tell the truth, I felt like stripping down and joining him."

Liz was telling Balbir about how Jim Tull got the man to put his clothes back on by singing along with him, when Larry spied Marcy Stoneman bearing down on the booth.

"Marcy?"

"Surprised?" She spat. "Think I was on the run like my jerk-off husband? No. He's with that rotten bitch Sandra."

"Jerry's wife?"

"Right! And Jerry wants to know if I want to run with him, because, hey, we're brothers, let's just swap wives. Say, you'll never notice the difference, we're used to passing the puck!" Marcy swelled with anger and Larry tried to calm her down.

"Okay. But you didn't."

"No way." Marcy leaned into Larry and stared up at his face. "I want to testify! I will tell you everything about that sleazy bastard and his schemes!" She poked Larry's chest. "I know where the bones are hid."

"Okay. Good. Suppose you come down to the station and make a statement?"

"Yes! I am ready." And Larry had no doubt that she was. Ready and determined.

"Okay," he said. "Let me call in and arrange things." Liz and Balbir stared at the scene, silent.

Larry closed and locked his car door. He had taken Marcy Stoneman to the station to wait for Jim Tull. Marcy had a fistful of notes and it looked like a lengthy interview was in store. Fran was making tea. Larry returned to LakeFest. "Kalmakoff!"

Larry turned around. "Yeah?"

Rebecca Grant came striding up. "Have you seen Janet Rimbert today?"

"Well..." Larry stalled.

"I need to see her. No, wait." Rebecca's hand flew to her face. "I mean, I have something to tell her." She held her fingers next to her mouth, thinking. "Or somebody."

"Sure," said Larry. He thought, if I wait long enough, Rebecca will talk herself into telling me what's so important.

"Oh!" Rebecca's hand flew from her face. "There she is!" She walked quickly between the trees onto the festival grounds. Larry could see Janet Rimbert in the distance, a short way from the booths. He watched from the trees as Rebecca went up to Janet and began talking. Rebecca's hands lifted, palms up, beseeching. Janet hunched over and stared at the ground, arms hanging like a sullen teenager being disciplined. She was a foot shorter than Rebecca before hunching over and now the other woman towered above her. Suddenly, Janet went bolt upright and pointed at Rebecca. She spat words through bared teeth and her eyes flashed. Rebecca recoiled and took a step back.

Then Pete Rimbert came out from behind the booths. Janet caught sight of him and turned back to

Rebecca and said something. Rebecca nodded as Janet walked over to Pete and the couple went back into the festival grounds together.

Larry made his way up toward the booths. Rebecca Grant saw him and turned into the crowd. She was gone when Larry caught up. What did I just witness, he wondered.

Larry stumbled through the day, drinking and passing a gallon or two of water. As the sun dropped behind the mountains his energy began to increase. He got a message from Tull: Marcy Stoneman knew nothing about the Blaney murder, but she had a lot to say about all the schemes that her husband and brother-in-law had planned. None ever worked out, so probably there were no charges to be brought against them, except the LakeFest robbery. Some while later, Larry got the word that Jerry Stoneman had been picked up trying to use a dead credit card, after he got belligerent with a cashier for refusing it. But Jack and Sandra were in the wind, as they say on television, and Larry could not quite picture them as murderers anyway. Marcy, now... But she was in custody, so nothing to do except his job.

The last act of the evening was on the stage, Scabpuller, a group from post-punk Seattle that once had a well-received album. Now, grey-haired and pot-bellied, wearing grunge uniform jeans and flannel shirts, they performed the songs of their youth. Soon, thought Larry. Soon, this day would be over with only one to go! The sun was long gone, the evening was cool, jacket or light sweater weather. Everything was as nice as could be. The group finished with their biggest hit. Back around 1992, *Rolling Stone* called the lyrics poetry, but tonight the distortion was so bad, Larry couldn't make out a word. There didn't seem to be an encore. He guided drunken, drugged, sunburned tourists to the parking lot or the camp grounds. He asked the people vomiting in the grass if they needed medical help. None did. Time to go home.

Larry opened his front door. The phone was ringing. He picked up and Danny Byron yelled in his ear, "There's another one! Another murder! Jesus, Larry, we need you back here!"

39

The body was stretched out in a small clearing in the trees past the north end of the stage. Larry recognized the plaid lumberjack shirt immediately. "Rebecca Grant?"

"Yeah," said Tull. "Now look at this." He squatted beside the corpse. "See? A bullet hole. Might be another one. Or even more. Her head is a mess."

"Looks like the shot went in at an angle." Larry calculated, looked back down the path. "That's funny... Rebecca was lying down when she was shot?"

"Maybe. We need the doctor to say what the exact angle was, but this wound looks consistent with her being face down on the ground and someone standing just over there," Jim gestured toward the edge of the clearing where Danny Byron was on his hands and knees, examining the grass. "Danny found a shell casing over there. I sent Phil over to the festival, Danny's got better eyes."

"Uh, right." Larry decided that this wasn't the moment to discuss Phil Plaskowitz and his abilities with Tull. "So Rebecca decided to take a nap and... I never figured her for a drinker."

"Maybe she wasn't. Maybe she was knocked down first."

Larry nodded. "Okay. We need the post-mortem." A thought struck him. "Who found the body?"

"A tourist taking a walk in the woods. He didn't say so, but I surmise that he was going to traffic some drugs with the couple that followed him right after and actually witnessed the dealer when he first caught sight of Rebecca. Which is probably a good thing, because otherwise I suspect that little weasel wouldn't had told anyone that he'd found a body." Jim Tull pointed back where Byron was searching. "He was standing over there when
he saw her."

"Yeah," said Larry. "There's a bit of a clearing here. Moon rose while the first big act was on. Tourists loved it, rising behind the mountains, above the stage. Anyway, there was some light here. Enough to see and shoot someone from that distance."

"So it seems. Well, one thing for certain," said Tull, "Marcy Stoneman didn't do it. She's still in custody, awaiting her lawyer, David Cantor."

"Oh. Guess she'll shut up after that."

"Yeah, Cantor will tell her to keep silent and by now she's probably calmed down enough to take his advice. Doesn't matter," said Tull, "I think she already told us everything she knew."

"Which wasn't much, really." Larry stared at Rebecca Grant's ruined skull. "Jim, why did you bring her up?"

"Marcy Stoneman?"

"Yeah. Why would she have anything to do with this?"

"I don't know, Larry. Maybe I've spent too much time in the sun. It's just... Never mind." Tull waved his hand in the air. It was beginning to get light and Larry could see the exhaustion in the man's face. He had slept no more than Larry had, maybe less.

"Today's the last day," Larry said. "Do we let all the tourists leave?"

"Yeah. Fran is going over the list of ticket buyers and Phil and Danny will be collecting names and addresses." Tull rubbed a hand over his face. "For what good it will do. Hell, anybody could have done this."

"But you figure somebody local."

"Well, yes. Someone local. Someone with a grudge. That's my theory."

Larry nodded. "Makes sense." He looked up at the brightening sky. "Lord, I'll be glad when this day is over." The sun climbed another inch past the mountains and the temperature rose another degree.

Danny Byron called out, "I found another one!" He held up a baggie with a shell casing in it.

As the day wore on, it clouded over and Larry was hoping it might rain and cool things down. Might be a thunder storm, lightning striking the stage: KeeRash! Equipment flying, amps exploding, prancing singer fried like a squirrel on a power line. He stifled the thought. It wasn't healthy. And the ordeal was almost over. Just a few more hours. Then he got a radio call from Fran. "Larry? There's a guy here who wants to confess to murder."

"Murder? You mean Rebecca Grant?"

"He's talking about a man he killed. I gave him a cup of tea and put him in the interview room."

"Okay. I'll be right down."

40

Larry sipped at his coffee. "You want more tea? Coffee? Water?"

The young man across the table shook his head. "No. I just... I just..." He spread his hands and shook his head.

"Okay. So you are John Dempster?"

"Yes."

"Also known as Johnny On The Spot."

"Yeah."

"Is that hyphenated?"

"What?"

"Is it Johnny hyphen On hyphen The hyphen Spot?" Larry drew the hyphens in the air with his finger. "Or maybe it's all one word, Johnnyonthespot?"

"I don't know. They said I needed a name so I got this one from a Ween song."

"Ween."

"Yeah, Gene and Dean Ween. Excellent group. An old group, but excellent." Johnny was twenty, officially an adult, but he looked younger to Larry.

"So, who said you needed a name?"

"Scabpuller. Joey himself told me."

"That would be," Larry looked at his notes, "Joey D. Shmoe?"

"Yeah. Joey the jerk, Joey Phony, Joey asshole..." Johnny was getting wound up. "Mister supposed-to-be-cool. You know how he spent his time?"

"Uh, groupies and drugs?"

"No! I was ready for that. It was just so..." Johnny sank his head into his hands. "And I knew they were old, but..."

Larry thought Scabpuller had broken up before Johnny was born. The group on stage had two members of the original six plus a drummer who had joined Scabpuller's second revival. The LakeFest performance was the first performance of Scabpuller v.2.5.

"He drank scotch. Okay. Scotch is okay. But it had to be special whiskey from some island somewhere and aged forever and cost a bundle and he never shared it." Johnny leaned across the table and stared into Larry's eyes. "He'd drink it while talking to his broker. His *broker*! Joey D. Shmoe had a *stockbroker*!" Johnny fell back in the chair. "This is the guy who wrote 'Capitalists Can Suck My Dick And Die'."

"How did you get to be a fan?"

"My dad. He said they were the greatest unknown band of the era. He said being unknown made them even greater. You know he was doing oxygen during the show?"

"Oxygen?"

" Yeah! Joey had a tank back of the amps and would run back and huff on it in between numbers or even during them! Like that creep in *Blue Velvet*."

"You listened to your dad's music?"

"Yeah. Specially after he went in the hospital. It was cassettes mostly. I had to find a player."

"Your dad was in the hospital?"

"Cancer. Pancreatic. He wasn't there long, then he died. We talked about music, the groups he wanted to start when he was young."

"So when you had a chance to play with Scabpuller..."

"Yeah! I thought it was great! I mean, I knew it wasn't going to be the same, but..." Johnny shook his head. "I never thought it would be so bad."

"So you were upset that Joey was spoiling his legacy."

"I don't know. Maybe. Something like that. I just didn't think he would be such a phony."

"Okay," said Larry, "Tell me about killing him."

"Well, I was... See, he wouldn't do the encore number. Said it was disrespectful."

"This was 'Capitalists Can Suck...'?"

"No. It was supposed to be 'Floating Turd'. You know, about politicians. But it turns out Joey is close to a guy in Congress, a Republican! Jesus! I mean, Libertarian, even Green, okay, but Republican? That's as bad as being a Democrat!"

"Right. So..."

"Then he said, fuck the encore. He said these shitkickers already got their money's worth. This was Scabpuller! They would play until people dragged them off the stage. They once did a six-hour concert. Wouldn't leave until the cops came on stage and cuffed them! Now, forty minutes and done."

"So you grabbed your Glock and..."

"I got my gun and looked around. Then I saw him over past the stage, walking into the trees. So I followed. I went along this trail and saw him, passed out on the ground. Too much fucking scotch!"

"So he was face down?"

"Yeah. Lying there. Fireworks going off." Johnny looked up. "Bastard made me miss the fireworks." He started to grin and Larry saw that Johnny was constructing a story around his actions, something he could tell his cellmates. He wanted to be cool.

Larry thought a second. "He was lying face down. How did you know it was him?"

"His shirt! He was wearing the lumberjack shirt that he wore on stage. And I could see his work boots. Work boots!" Johnny snarled. "He wore a suit when he met with his broker. A suit! With a goddam necktie!"

"Right," said Larry, "Well..." He pondered what to say next.

"I don't care," said Johnny. "I'll plead guilty and be proud that I removed this jerk. Anyway, my dad said everybody that's worth anything has gone to jail for a while."

"Your dad?"

"WTO riots," Johnny said proudly, "Or G-8. One of those. Charged with conspiracy to commit violence or something like that. They reduced the charges to criminal mischief or something so he only got time served while waiting for trial. Dad did do some time for other stuff, though, property crimes, theft from rich people who could afford it. Some drug stuff." Johnny shrugged. "The usual crimes they pin on the underclass to keep them down."

"Well, you're confessing to murder..."

"Yes." Johnny raised his chin a little higher. "I did it." He was proud.

Larry decided to end this. "The person you shot, the one lying on the ground, that was a local woman, Rebecca Grant."

"Woman..?" Johnny's face crumpled. "What..?"

"Yeah. She wore a plaid shirt, too." Larry started to add something sarcastic about how Joey D. Shmoe was still alive to clip stock coupons, but Johnny turned completely white and suddenly vomited all over the table.

There was silence for a minute, then Larry said, "Let us clean that up. You have to stay here for a while.

Look, you need a lawyer, okay?" Johnny just stared at him. Larry grabbed the phonebook. "Here. There's only a couple that are close." The directory listed every landline in an area about three hundred miles in diameter. Larry tapped David Cantor's name. "This guy is local legal aid."

"Okay," said Johnny. "Okay." He began to cry. "I really fucked up, didn't I?"

On his way out, Larry told Fran, "Call David Cantor. Tell him a prisoner is asking for him."

Fran arched her eyebrows. "Really?"

"Yes!" Larry was out of patience. "Call him." Larry turned in the doorway. "Fran, that body that went to the coroner, call me right away if there's a medical report. Okay?"

Fran, speaking into the phone, nodded and waved Larry off.

41

"Jim, I think we need to know exactly what happened here."

"I agree, Larry. Danny said..." He waved over his shoulder toward Danny Byron, still on his hands and knees, poking through the weeds. Phil Plaskowitz had joined him, hunting through the brush. "Danny said, maybe some of the tourists got a picture. They might even be able to use their cellphones for that, even if they can't send the pictures on-line."

"Fireworks." Larry said, "That's when she was shot. Everyone would have cameras pointed at the fireworks, with the moon up over the lake, not over here in the trees."

Jim rolled a cigar between his fingers. He asked gently, "You know that Rebecca was killed then? During the fireworks?"

Larry held up a hand. "I didn't say 'killed', I said 'shot'. We have to get the medical report back, but..."

"Yeah," said Tull. He lit his cigar.

"Damn it! I should have gotten Fran to call the doc... What's his name? To ask for a quick opinion on... on..."

"On whether Rebecca's head was beaten in before she was shot. And can he tell us, quickly before he cuts her open and examines her last meal and weighs her liver and all those other things that will take days to do, can he tell us quickly the cause of death. If possible." Jim drew on his cigar. "I already did that. So we should get a preliminary finding pretty soon. I expect he will tell us that Rebecca had her head bashed in before being shot. But I don't know if he can say which actually caused her death. But maybe..."

Larry started to laugh. "Lord, Jim! You are amazing!"

"You bet your ass. I told him that what he told us could prevent having to detain everyone at the Fest and maybe check their cellphones. Thousands of American tourists. The province would be billed." Tull gestured with his cigar. "And I told him this was a preliminary opinion that would not be evidence but only used to further the investigation. Oh, I fed him a lot of shit." He puffed at the cigar. "And I told him that the responsibility was all mine and the mayor's..."

"Did you ask Wolichuk..?"

"Of course not. Now quit laughing before one us collapses in hysterics."

"Okay, okay." Larry turned and looked up into the forest. "I think Danny had the right idea. We need an eyewitness."

"Good plan. I wonder if any music lovers live up the mountain there."

"Maybe," said Larry. "It's possible there might be. Think I'll take a look."

Jim Tull smiled, shrugged, and stuck his cigar back in his face.

Larry walked up into the trees. Below him, he could see the spot where Rebecca's body had been discovered. Danny Byron was still poking around, looking for evidence. Larry climbed up higher and cast around until he found a spot above an old slide where the trees opened a little. He sat on a fallen log. He had a clear view of the stage. An earnest young couple was just finishing an acoustic set. There was a scattering of applause. People milled about. There was still an hour and a half or so before the main acts came on. And he could see the clearing, Danny working, Jim standing, hands on hips, looking up in his direction. A ska band took the stage, already sweating in their rude-boy dark suits. Larry noticed an empty wine bottle by his feet. Royal Red.

"Larry! Where you going?"

"Be back soon, Jim. Just going to get some wine."

"What?" Tull stared after Larry's car and shook his head. "Maybe gone crazy in the heat," he muttered.

"No way," said Plaskowitz, "Not Larry."

"You're quite the booster now, aren't you?" said Tull. "Since Larry said good things about you."

Plaskowitz clamped his mouth shut and stared into the trees. Finally he said, "Larry's a good cop."

"Yeah, well, I agree on that one, Phil. I do agree," said Tull. "So we'll find out what he's up to eventually, I guess."

Danny Byron joined them. "Look what I found." He held up a plastic bag. Inside was a Fest-A-Rod. There was blood on it.

42

"Fran, anything happen?"

"Yes, Larry. Cantor is in talking to his client now." She frowned at him. "Quite the mess you left for me to clean up. Usually I get Plaskowitz to do stuff like that, but he's too good a cop now to sully his hands with..."

"Fran! I'm sorry. Next time I'll clean up, okay?"

"All right. Don't get your hackles up."

"Sorry. But it's been a long week."

"Sure. But it's almost over. We could all use some sleep." Fran paused. "I called the doctor examining Rebecca's body. He hasn't finished the autopsy, hadn't started really, but he did take a look and said, based on what he'd seen so far, that Rebecca Grant died from massive head trauma. Blunt object-type trauma."

"Right!"

"And he thinks the fatal blows were struck before she was shot. There were pieces of skull smashed into the brain, so she was dead by the time the bullet struck her. Part of the brain was exposed, the skull already gone, when she was shot." Fran made a face. "Full report tomorrow, maybe."

"Okay." Larry glanced up at the door to the interview room. "I guess I should wait before telling Johnny he shot a corpse. Get the full report first." Larry sighed. "Poor bastard thinks he murdered a woman."

"He could have."

"But he didn't. Okay." Larry knocked on the door, then stuck his head into the interview room. Cantor rose up out of his chair, pointed his finger at Larry's chest, and started in on having his interview interrupted. Larry raised his hand. "I'm not here to question your client, Counsellor, I have a piece of information for you." He looked at Johnny. "We think Rebecca Grant was already dead when you shot her."

"What? Then release my client immediately!"

Larry shook his head. "Come on, Cantor, there's going to be some kind of charge – talk to Crown Counsel about that – and your client is at minimum a material witness to murder. And anyway, he's transient so I'm not letting him go on his own recognizance."

Cantor tried to argue but Larry shut the door to the interview room. "I probably shouldn't have done that."

"No," said Fran, "You're a complete marshmallow, Larry."

"Right. Well, I got to hit the liquor store."

"What?"

"Yeah. Get some wine."

43

It was just getting dark as Larry quietly made his way through the brush and came up from behind the fallen tree above the stage area. He could see a silhouetted figure sitting on the log. "Hi, Marvin."

"Oh, hey, Officer."

Larry sat on the log near Marvin. He set down a half gallon jug of Royal Red between them. "Good view from here."

"It's not illegal."

"Of course not! This is Crown Land, belongs to the people. People like you, Marvin." Marvin didn't say anything. "Brought some wine. Want any?"

Larry unscrewed the cap and took a sip from the jug. The wine was thick and so sweet it made his teeth ache. He set down the jug and Marvin picked it up and took a swig. "That's good." He took another drink. "How'd you know my brand?"

"Saw the empty you left up here last night."

"Oh. Last night."

"Yeah." Larry raised the jug, took a small sip and passed it back. "I guess you saw what happened."

Marvin didn't answer right away. He drank some more wine. Finally he said, "Will I have to testify?"

"I don't think so. But I can't promise." Marvin had deserted from the US Army in 1971 after getting orders for Vietnam. He had lived in the bush ever since. There had been several amnesties over the years, but Marvin had stayed in hiding. He was probably safe from prosecution, but Immigration might deport him, depending on whether the federal government was in tough or soft mode. Larry figured that the man had grown to like his hermit outlaw existence. "The thing is, you tell me what happened, then I can use that information to dig up enough evidence so we can proceed without you."

Marvin took another drink. The light from the stage reflected from his wispy white hair. Larry thought he was about seventy years old. He expected to hear, one winter, that hikers or hunters had discovered Marvin's body. The shack Marvin had built for himself had pretty thin walls and Larry had asked, once or twice, if Marvin might want to come into town during the coldest months, but such questions made Marvin nervous and Larry quit asking.

A hip-hop group was on stage now. Rumor had it that the singer was involved in the murder of another rapper, but maybe that was just a story dreamed up by publicists. Larry couldn't understand how being called a murderer was good publicity, but there was a lot he was resigned to never understanding. It was a strange world. "You like this music?"

"Not usually. Sometimes. I heard some Grandmaster Flash that was cool, but this... I don't know." Marvin drank some more. "Sometimes, late at night, when things are right, I get radio that isn't CBC." Marvin shook his head. "I don't understand a lot of it. I've been listening to classical, too. Don't understand that either."

"How'd you like Scabpuller?"

"They were okay. Short set, though."

"I guess it was after they finished when you saw what you saw."

Marvin pulled on the bottle. His speech was beginning to slur and Larry took the wine from him and pretended to drink.

Finally, Marvin said, "I kept thinking they would come back, do an encore, but nope." Marvin slowly shook his head.

"Then you saw..."

"Well, she came down the path, Rebecca Grant."

"You knew her?"

"Oh, yeah. She got all up in my face once about leghold traps. I told her, I don't use steel traps at all. I set snares sometimes. She said you use wire? I said yes but that don't make it a steel trap. Does it?" Marvin drew a breath. "Thought it best not to talk about the difference between legholds and snares, because..."

"Marvin?"

"Right. Well, she didn't know the difference, I think." Marvin paused. "If there's some wire in a snare, that doesn't make it a steel trap, does it?"

"Not in my book."

"No. But she couldn't let go of it, kept after me. I was real sorry I came into town that day."

"Uh-huh," said Larry. "So you saw her down in the clearing there."

"Yeah. She was walking this way. Then she turned around and was yelling at this person following her. I couldn't really see them at first, not till they moved down the path a little. They argued a while, then Rebecca Grant turned back down the path and that's when it happened. Wham! Wham! Wham! I never saw anything like that before." Marvin stared off into the distance. Larry passed him the jug and Marvin took a deep drink. "Then after, right after, the fireworks start going, and that was strange, because I kept looking up at the fireworks and down at her body and up at the fireworks and..."

"Marvin?"

"Well, it was something I couldn't control, you know? And I couldn't help looking up. I mean, I'm not a bad person, to look away from a murder, like that one in New York, Kitty..."

"Marvin?"

"But I was looking down at her when the kid comes up. I saw him down the path there, this kid comes up and shoots her. I mean why? She wasn't going anywhere. I think she was dead. But he hauls out this pistol. Bang! Bang! That was what happened, wham wham wham and bang bang. I left then. All this stuff going on, I forgot to clean up my wine bottle. I always clean up my mess. Sometimes I clean up after campers, too. You don't want trash all over."

"No," said Larry, "You don't. Can you describe the person that hit Rebecca Grant?"

"Oh, I knew who it was. Had a run in with them both, that pair! Both of 'em mad about something or other I did they didn't like. Something I did after I drank some wine, I think. I mean, I stepped around back where nobody could see me and nobody uses that building anyway..."

"Marvin!"

"Yeah, well pissing on a wall, out back where nobody can see you should not be a big deal to people." Marvin looked Larry straight in the eye like he was daring him to disagree. Larry reached for the wine jug.

"May I?"

"Oh, sure, yes. Where are my manners? And you brought the wine, too!"

"So. About these..."

"Yep. I remember. Disliked them both. A piece of work, both of them!" Then Marvin told Larry who murdered Rebecca Grant.

Larry stared down at the stage. "Another act will be coming out soon, maybe one you like better."

"Maybe. Anyway, there's the fireworks later. I want to see them."

"Yeah," said Larry, "Whether the music is any good or not, the fireworks are always worth watching."

44

"Well, aren't you looking perky," said Tull, "Got something?"

"Jim, I've got Rebecca's killer. And, I think, Doug Blaney's."

"Two killers?"

"No," said Larry, "Same one but I don't have... Is that Marcy Stoneman? Over there with the Rimberts?"

"Yeah," said Tull. "We let her go. Charged with the LakeFest theft. That's preliminary charges and I don't know if they'll stick. Anyway, released on her own recognizance. Larry, you saying she did it? Because Fran is pretty clear..."

"No, Jim, not her." Larry walked over to the group. "Janet. Where's your Fest-A-Rod?"

"What?" Janet Rimbert stepped toward Larry, fists clenched.

"Pete has his, but you seem to have lost yours." Pete Rimbert stared at his Fest-A-Rod like it was something that had just appeared in his hand.

"I lost it somewhere! Anyway, what difference does it make to you? You wouldn't make the security people carry them, so why should I carry one?"

Pete Rimbert looked up from his Fest-A-Rod and glared right into Larry's eyes. He gripped the rod tighter and raised it a little. Larry suddenly realized that he wasn't wearing his gun. He spoke very quietly. "Pete, lower that weapon. Don't make Jim shoot you."

Jim Tull fiddled with his holster, taking his time as he watched Pete Rimbert slowly lower the Fest-A-Rod.

Larry breathed out. "Okay. Janet Rimbert, you are under arrest for the murder of Rebecca Grant." He dropped a hand on her shoulder. "Come quietly, Janet, and I won't have to cuff you."

45

"Well, she confessed."

"Kind of thought she would," said Jim Tull. "Plea deal?"

"Yeah," said Larry, Second-degree murder for both. Rebecca's was the hard part to defend. If she'd only murdered Doug Blaney, she might have gotten off with a slap on the wrist."

"Yeah. Or a medal. If she hadn't bashed Doug's head in from behind, she could've pleaded self-defense and gotten off easy. But Rebecca found out about the bloody butt wipes and then she knew. Janet just couldn't pass up grabbing that free stuff. And then she was killed. From behind." Jim Tull shook his head.

"She almost told me, I think," said Larry, "But Rebecca always had to work things out, figure out what side she was on."

"Yeah. She was always arguing with herself. Well, I guess she confronted Janet and Janet figured she needed to be taken out," said Tull. He was wearing a bathrobe and underwear shorts. He was barefoot. Everybody on the force had taken three full days off, in turn, to recover from LakeFest. Jim Tull was the last in the rotation. He was in about Hour Twenty-six of his Seventy-two and reeked of booze.

Larry was very conscious that he was disrupting Tull's down-time. He got up to go. "So I thought I'd let you know about the confession."

"Why, thank you. Don't go, Larry. Sit and chat a while. Can I fix you a drink? Or a beer?"

"Okay. A beer."

Tull leaned over the arm of his easy chair and opened the fridge that stood next to him. He extracted a bottle of beer and closed the fridge door in one practised motion. "Here you go."

"Thanks, Jim."

Jim Tull lived in a one-room plus indoor bathroom log house just outside town. The one room held a wood stove, a sound system, and a fold-out chesterfield besides the fridge and easy chair. Tull's uniform was draped over a television set where he'd thrown it. Books were piled on the floor around the chair and the chesterfield. Larry recognized some of the authors' names, though he didn't know their books. Mishima, Beckett, Naipaul, who had died and been in the news. Larry had seen a movie made from a Cormac McCarthy novel.

"Did Janet say anything more about her motivation?"

Larry shrugged. "Not really. I think she already said it all. The Crown thinks there was some kind of lesbian relationship here that might involve all three women. But they've got it wrong."

"Yeah. You had it right at the beginning, you said somebody just wanted to help."

"That's what Janet told Crown Counsel, she said she wanted to help Mildred. I talked to him on the phone. I said, besides that, you have to understand Doug Blaney was the kind of guy who could rouse murderous rage in anyone who spoke to him for more than thirty seconds. But he's still into this sex thing."

"Academic now, unless her lawyer can use it to get a lighter sentence." Tull waved around his free hand, the one not holding his drink. "So who was Janet's lawyer that negotiated this deal?"

"I don't know. Guy from the Okanagan somewhere. She really wanted Crane Baxter to represent her."

Jim Tull snorted. "Not a chance in hell. One way you get to be a lawyer who's never lost a case, is to never take a losing case."

"So he's really not that good? Just picks his clients well?"

"Oh, no, Baxter is good enough, especially on civil stuff. That's why I got him to write my contract."

"Your contract?"

"Yeah," said Tull, "You never heard about it?"

"No."

"Thought Fran would have told you by now." Tull shook his head. "You never know."

Larry didn't think about it, he just felt the question slip past his lips. "Why does Fran dislike you, Jim?"

Tull laughed. "Because of the contract. Ha!" He sipped some of his drink. "You see, Fran is a romantic."

"Okay."

"So I was Chief, newly appointed, and there were rumors that the mill was about to close and everyone was on edge. The Mayor then – his name was Gummidge! I swear to Christ! Gummidge! – Anyway, he was facing a tricky situation. A lot of Council members had resigned and moved away, but there were enough left so they could form a quorum. Gummidge was getting less interested in being the mayor by the minute and he was worried that, one thing and another might come out during the inevitable inquisition on why and how he allowed everybody to be out of work."

"What might come out?"

"I'm not completely sure. Some stock scams, a few of them, but that's only a guess based on meticulous investigation by a professional law officer. Namely, me!" Tull grinned and Larry realized the man was very drunk. "Anyway, I uncovered that much, but there was probably more."

"Okay. So Gummidge wanted to leave town to avoid having his dealings looked at too closely. Seriously? Wait, was there a connection to the mill closing?"

"Not exactly. What would come out in the stock investigation was that Gummidge had shorted mill stock."

"He knew the mill was going to shut down? Was it insider trading?"

Tull shrugged. "Maybe. I don't know. It would need some professional business lawyers and investigators to put a case together. But he got rich, somehow, pretty quick. And then he came to me."

"About the stock case?"

"Nope." Tull rooted around and found a cigar. "Well, I suppose that was unsaid. He wanted me to stay quiet about the stock thing – I mean, suppose people found out he'd bet on the mill closing? They'd lynch him!" Tull lit his cigar. "But what he really wanted was to take my wife along when he left town."

"What?"

"Yeah, I thought it was pretty strange, too. Kind of Victorian, like, 'Sir, may I have your wife's hand?' or something. But Gummidge saw it as one big package: the stock deal, Arlene, and a clean getaway. I'm not sure what it was he thought I could do to mess things up. Go after my wife, maybe? That's what Fran would expect. And Arlene had her name on some of the stock stuff. Gummidge used her as a cat's-paw, now he wanted to save her. Kind of sweet, you know?" Tull drew on his cigar. "Well, Arlene and I had already gotten past the point where we could tolerate each other. We hardly spoke any more. Anyway, I could tell anyone I wanted to about Gummidge's stock deals, if I wanted. I never signed a non-disclosure or anything. So, I said okay, but you have to do something for me." Tull blew a perfect smoke ring. "So I gave them twenty-four hours and then called RCMP. I sent everything I had to commercial crimes division. Never heard any more about it." Tull paused. "Never asked, either."

"Okay, but what was it?"

"What?"

"The thing Gummidge had to do for you."

"Oh. Well. Pay for Crane Baxter to write a contract for me that no one can break."

"You mean the city can't fire you?"

"Oh, they can always get a contract with the Mounties and get rid of me that way. But, no, they cannot fire me." Tull grinned. "My job is sacrosanct. I have been sanctified by the great Crane Baxter. Of course, I do not have hiring powers, either." He looked closely at Larry. "You know about that? People left and

Council wouldn't authorize funds to get somebody to replace them. I thought you would ask Fran why there are no new hires and she would explain the contract to you."

"No. I thought we never hired anyone new because there wasn't any money."

"Money! Hell, those greedy assholes are making a fortune off of us! We do the work of fifteen people and they pay us crap wages and then bitch about it! They wanted to claim Byron and Plaskowitz were part-time and not pay benefits!"

"Lord, Jim, take it easy!"

"Okay, okay. But it does piss me off that I can't pay you guys better or get some of the resources that we need. It's the contract. Sorry." Tull wiped his hand down his face and Larry saw how exhausted the man was. "Anyway, that's why Fran hates me. Because I traded my wife for this lousy job."

Larry pondered for a minute. "But why, Jim? Why did you want this job here?"

"It seemed like a good place to be. It's quiet and the lake and the forest and mountains are good to be around. It's a good place to be to watch everything unravel."

"What? Unravel? You a survivalist, that kind of thing?"

"No. Jesus! Most of those assholes couldn't survive a power outage. Anyway, who wants to live in a bunker?" He drained his glass. "But, sure, it's all unravelling." Tull grinned. "Or I am. Either way, this is a good place to be."

46

"That one looks like a guy with a sun for his head." Said Balbir.

"Yeah," said Larry, "Maybe he was brighter than the other guys."

Balbir almost smiled a little. His breath made clouds in the autumn air. Yellow lines spidered down the mountains tracing the stream courses lined by birch and alder trees that had turned color.

"It's getting cold," said Larry. "Let's head back."

They had gone for an end-of-summer picnic. Anusheela had brought samosas and Larry brought sausage rolls. Balbir refused the samosas, ate the sausage rolls, hardly said a word. He had been withdrawn ever since Larry moved in. Anusheela seemed to be perpetually irritated with her son, her lips were drawn tight and there was a crease forming between her eyes. Larry tried to chat up Balbir and managed to get him to walk over to the Standing Stone and look at the petroglyphs, deer, fish, and humanoid figures carved into the rock long ago. The Stone stood up thirty feet tall on the narrow valley floor.

"How did they put this here?"

"Who?"

"The people that did these pictures," said Balbir, "How did they get this stone here?"

Then Larry understood that Balbir saw the Standing Stone, a great block of granite, as a monument. "Uh, I think it was already here. The glaciers brought it down in the Ice Age."

"Oh," said Balbir.

"I never thought of it like that," said Larry, "Like something people set up for a purpose. I thought this was where folks left a message or a sign or maybe even their name."

"Like those guys." Balbir pointed to the spray-painted names from the Arcadia High School Class of 1993.

"Maybe more than that. People say that they recorded dreams here. Maybe they came here on a vision quest and then recorded their dreams."

"They dreamed about deer? And fish?"

"Yeah, well, that was important. That was food."

"Yeah, people shoot deer here all the time. You don't have to dream much."

"Okay," said Larry, defeated.

"Dreams?" Balbir pointed at the "Graduates!" sign. "They had dreams. Until the town fell apart."

"Right. Okay," said Larry. "Let's head on back." All at once, he felt very old.

"This year," said Balbir, "I want to have Christmas." He crossed his arms on his chest.

"We had Christmas last year," said Anusheela, "And the year before."

"This year we do it right."

"Humph," said Anusheela. They were steering toward a fight.

"I love Christmas," said Larry. They were sitting around Anusheela's kitchen table where the three had shared an extra large frozen pizza with everything.

"Good. We will have a Canadian Christmas," said Balbir, "A Christian will show us." Arms crossed, he smiled at his mother.

"I don't go to church that much…" Actually, Larry didn't go at all. "So maybe Canadian Christmas and Christian Christmas aren't the same."

"Tell us then the difference," said Anusheela. She was nettled and upset.

"Well," Larry gathered his thoughts, "Not speaking for Christians but just for me, Christmas is a big party right when you shouldn't have one. I mean, you know things are going to get worse. There's going to be more snow and it's going to get colder, cold enough sometimes so the trees freeze and you hear them in the night cracking. Pow! And then even when it gets warmer all that snow thaws and refreezes and there's mud and… Well, Christmas comes right at the beginning of the worst time of the year." Larry shook his head. Balbir and Anusheela were leaning toward him. "And the days are short. You get up in the dark, you go to work, the sun comes up a little after, just gray light though, the sun is weak. Then, about three, you look up and the sun is setting and it gets dark and you go home in the dark. But," Larry held a finger in the air, "But at Christmas the days start to get a little longer and that's the one thing, you know you've turned some kind of corner, the light is coming back and things will get better eventually, even though you've got three miserable months to go. So, you throw a party, a big party, and everybody celebrates! They eat too much and they drink too much and they spend too much money and do stupid silly things and it's all kind of defiance. It's saying, 'Come on, show me the worst you got, I'm laughing at you.'"

"Who? God?"

"No, not God. This setup, the deal that humans get here on Earth. That's what we're defying. We're saying, 'I can take the worst there is and still party!' Because, you know what? Life is still pretty good. No matter how bad it sometimes gets." Larry's voice ran down. He realized that Balbir and Anusheela were hanging on his words. "Well, that's just me. I don't know."

Balbir broke the silence. "We will have a Christmas tree?"

"Well, of course!" Larry waved a hand. "The woods are full of trees! We'll go out one day and find the perfect one. We'll cut it down and bring it home and put lights and stuff all over it." And then it will fall over, thought Larry, like the damn things always do. But that would be fun, too.

"Yes," breathed Balbir, his eyes full of Christmas lights.

"But that's a ways off. We've got Thanksgiving first. And Halloween!"

"And Diwali!" said Anusheela.

"Oh, man!" Balbir groaned.

"Diwali? Another party?"

"Yes, with many lights because it comes when things are getting darker, as you said. So we have lights and colours and sweet things to eat. Barfi!"

"Barfy?" From the corner of his eye, Larry caught Balbir tensing up. A memory flashed through his brain. He was ten or eleven and in his mother's kitchen. Two of his friends were there, too, one of the few times non-Russians had ever come into his house, and his mother was serving them all borscht. She sat down the bowls full of shredded cabbage, bits of tomato, carrot slices like golden coins gleaming through the white potato soup. He sprinkled crisp shiny squares of chopped green pepper over his bowl and took a big spoonful just as one of his friends snickered, "It looks like barf." And the other boy laughed. And that sweet soup, rich with butter and cream, all turned to bile in his throat, a memory so strong he could taste it now.

"…pistachios," Anusheela was saying, "But now you can get them from California and I like to mix them with the almonds…"

"There's always room for another holiday," said Larry, "And I love pistachios."

"Oh, everyone does," said Anusheela. "Barfi is very sweet, though, maybe too sweet."

"Like Nanaimo bars," said Larry.

"Yes! Exactly like that!"

"Too sweet can be really good. Sometimes too much is just enough."

Anusheela laughed. And so did Balbir! Only a little, but he laughed. And each of them, just for a moment, caught the same notion, or at least a hint of it: Maybe this can work. The three of us. Maybe it can work. No one voiced the thought. Instead they talked about food and holidays and Balbir stayed up way past his bedtime, animated and talking. Outside, the sky was perfectly clear, a billion stars brilliant against the black night, and that clear sky meant it was going to be cold, maybe the first hard frost of the year. The season of celebration was at hand.

THE END